TED AND TIME-TRAVELLING TOILET

SHAKESPEARE SHAKE-UP

Tedeo & Chloliet

BY
STEVEN VINACOUR

AWARD PUBLICATIONS LIMITED

For Marshall

A book lover and a gentleman

ISBN 978-1-78270-473-7

Text copyright © 2022 Steven Vinacour
Illustrations by James Cottell
This edition copyright © Award Publications Limited

The right of Steven Vinacour to be identified as the author
of this work has been asserted in accordance with the
Copyright, Designs and Patents Act 1988.

First published by Award Publications Limited 2022

Published by Award Publications Limited,
The Old Riding School, Welbeck,
Worksop, S80 3LR

 /awardpublications @award.books @award_books
www.awardpublications.co.uk

22-1006 1

Printed in the United Kingdom

MIX
Paper from
responsible sources
FSC® C171272

WARNING:
CONTAINS TOILET HUMOUR!

CHAPTER 1

I am a TREE.
 Shhhh!

I am on the floor, crouched into a tight ball.
I am bunched up so tightly that my knees
are pressed to my nose. My knees smell
funny. I didn't know that knees even had a
smell but mine do and they smell funny (not
funny like HAHA but funny as in YEUCH).

My mind wanders from being a tree and
I start to consider what knees taste like. I
stick my tongue out and have a taste. They

taste **salty** and **EARTHY.** Probably because I was playing football on the field at lunchtime and I fell over. I don't think I'll do that again. (Lick my knees, that is — not play football... or fall over. I mean, I don't want to fall over but I probably will. The chances of going my whole life without ever falling over again are slim.)

Knees don't taste as good as elbows. Did you know that all elbows taste like *strawberries?*

Go on, try it. Have a taste of your own elbow...

HAHAHA! GOT YOU! You can't do it can you? Because it's ***impossible*** to lick your own elbows.

(Aha! Don't believe me, eh? Go on, try again.)

You see. It's impossible!

If you tried this at home and you are

reading this on your own then it's a bit amusing, but if you are in the library or, better still, in a bookshop deciding if you should buy this book*, now all the other customers think you're strange because you have your tongue out and are trying to lick your own elbows, then THAT IS HILARIOUS! (*You should.)

I'm just going to sit here a moment and imagine you in a crowded bookshop, trying to lick your elbow.

Wait... haha

Wait, not done yet... HAHA!

Hang on, still imagining it... HAHAHA!

OK, carry on... no wait...

HAHA!

OK, ready now. Continue.

Now you know *that's* impossible. However, it is possible to lick someone else's elbow – but I wouldn't recommend it unless you know them *really* well and you get them to agree to it, perhaps in writing.

The TOP 5 places I wouldn't recommend trying to lick a stranger's elbow

- In a queue at the supermarket (although you could always claim you were hungry).

- In the cinema (unless the film is very boring).

- In a doctor's surgery (very unwise – especially if you don't know why they're visiting the doctor).

- In the swimming pool (this is just super weird and likely to get you arrested).

- In the police station after being

arrested at the swimming pool.

SCENE: In a prison. The prisoners stand in a line

Prisoner 1: (*steps forward*) I'm Dave, I robbed a bank.

Prisoner 2: (*steps forward*) I'm Bill, I stole a car.

Prisoner 3 (Me): (*steps forward*) I'm Terry Barry Larry Gary Harry Jerry Perry Lenny Benny Johnny Tommy Julie, and I licked a stranger's elbow in a public swimming pool.

Prisoner 1: That's a weird name.

Prisoner 2 (Me): Really? After what I just told you, you think my name is the weird part?

Right, where was I?

9

Oh yes, I'm a **TREE.** I'm in drama class and everyone is pretending to be a tree. It's not the first time that our *drama teacher*, Mr Peters, has made us pretend to be a tree. He lowers his glasses down his nose and peers over them at us, muttering things like *'good'*, and *'excellent'*. He rubs his small goatee beard. He looks like he is thinking but to be honest I don't think he is that interested in our interpretation of what a tree looks like in human form. I just think that it is his go-to lesson if he **FORGETS** to prepare a proper lesson for us.

It's all very quiet as we very slowly start to move. We all imagine the sun coming out, making us grow. We stretch out our arms as if they are branches. Weird, creepy branches with hands and fingers on

10

the end. Suddenly, **Martin Harris,** the school bully, jumps up and starts *SCREAMING* and running around the drama hall. Mr Peters immediately pushes his glasses back up to where they should be and yells at him, '**Martin Harris!** What on **earth** do you think you are doing?'

'I'm a tree... **AAAARRRGGHH!**' he shouts, running around and flapping his arms. '...I'm a tree in the middle of a hurricane.'

A couple of people started to giggle. Mr Peters told him to wait outside the room until he'd calmed down and stopped being so silly.

Mr Peters is one of my favourite teachers. A rumour went around school last term that his first name is

Peter. I wasn't sure if it was true but I started to tell people that his middle name was Peter, too. Then I told everyone that his full name is Mr Peter Peter Peters Jnr because I liked the idea that his dad was called Mr Peter Peter Peters and he was so happy with his name that he gave his son the same name. Although none of it is true. STAGE MOUNT SCHOOL is the kind of place that loves a ridiculous rumour and they will literally believe anything.

I carry on growing and stretching, pretending my arms are branches swaying in the wind. I am very good at being a TREE. We are all slowly getting to full height when Mr Peters opens the door and tells Martin Harris to come back in and behave himself. He walks through the room shouting 'TIMBER!' and pushing people over. Mr Peters sighs, opens the door and tells Martin to leave the room again.

Mr Peters wanders amongst us and points out who is doing a good job. He nods to me and tells me *'well done,'* and, *'think about how the tree feels when the sun comes out or the rain falls on its leaves'*. I nod enthusiastically but don't give his suggestion any more thought. I think being a tree is pointless, but Mr Peters tells us that it's one of the most important exercises to master in drama. I've watched lots of dramas on the television and as yet have never seen anyone pretending to be a tree – although I did once see a dog who liked to bark.

HAHA! It's a tree joke... because of the bark... and the dog... oh, never mind!

When we are all standing up as tall as we can get, trying to keep our balance on our tiptoes with our fingers outstretched, wiggling like leaves, Mr Peters tells us how GREAT we all are and then asks us to form a semi-circle around him with our chairs as he has an important announcement to make.

'Right, listen carefully, class. I have a very exciting announcement. This afternoon I will be posting up a sheet on the school noticeboard with details of this year's school show. If you would like to audition, then write your name on the sheet and I will let you know when and where the auditions will be held. There was a little buzz of excitement from some of my class. Sandra Wum (AKA Sandy Bum) put her hand up.

'Yes, Sandra.'

'What show will we, like, be performing? Is it **FROZEN?** I would, like, make a fabulous Elsa.'

'No! Please pick somebody else-a! **ANYBODY ELSE-A!**' piped up Martin Harris (which was a surprisingly good joke for him).

'Yes, thank you, Martin!' snapped Mr Peters. 'In fact, this year's show will be the Shakespeare classic, *Romeo & Juliet*. We are looking for the best actors and actresses in the school. So, if you think you can act then sign up and audition. It will be a lot of fun.'

Everyone in the class groaned.

'And you will miss lessons during rehearsals,' said Mr Peters with a sly grin.

'YAAAAAAYY!' We all cheered.

I turned to my best friend, Ollie. 'Well,

that's me out then. I can't act.'

'You were pretty good at being a tree. I was convinced.'

'Ollie, seriously, I was standing up and waving my arms around. You weren't convinced I was a tree.'

'Yes, I was,' he argued. 'If I were a dog, I would've cocked my leg and had a wee on you.'

'That's comforting to know, thank you, Ollie.'

'It would be the perfect opportunity to impress Chloe,' he pointed out.

OK, WAIT! Hold everything. I need to explain something. Chloe is the most beautiful girl in the school. I thought we were getting on really well, we even went to the school prom together and were crowned prom king and queen, but lately she hasn't been talking to me much. She does this A LOT. Before you say it, it doesn't mean she doesn't think I'm super funny and handsome and awesome! It's just how Chloe is sometimes (always). I know I didn't do anything wrong because I asked her and she told me not to be silly. I don't think I fully understand Chloe, but it doesn't matter as long as one day she agrees to be my wife. We will sort it all out then I'm sure. In the meantime, if she doesn't want to be my girlfriend, then I would settle for us getting the lead roles in *Romeo & Juliet* and then at least she'd pretend to be my girlfriend and then once she's experienced what it's like having me as her pretend actor-boyfriend then she will definitely want us to be together for real. That's it, Bob's your uncle.

(Just so that you know, 'Bob's your uncle' is a saying. I don't actually have an Uncle Bob but I do have an Uncle Tom who is very tall and smells of petrol. Incidentally, the saying Bob's your uncle dates back to 1887 when British Prime Minister Robert 'Bob' Cecil gave an important role to his nephew and people weren't happy about it and thought he only got the job because Bob was his uncle. That's interesting right? No? Really?! Well I thought it was, so there!)

OK, time to draw up a to do list...

TO DO LIST
Draw up To Do list ✓
Add my name to the list ✓

TED JONES' TO DO LIST
Draw up To Do list ✓
Add my name to the list ✓
Get the role of *Romeo*

(and make sure Chloe gets the role of *Juliet*.

I don't want Sandra 'Sandy Bum' Wum getting the

role because I'll have to kiss her and then I'll

end up marrying her or something equally awful.)

Marry Chloe (not Sandra)
Stop writing To Do list ✓
Go to the next chapter ✓

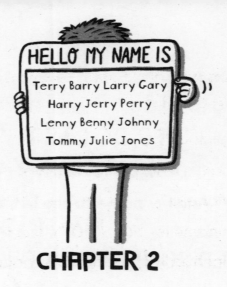

HELLO MY NAME IS

Terry Barry Larry Gary
Harry Jerry Perry
Lenny Benny Johnny
Tommy Julie Jones

CHAPTER 2

After our **drama** lesson, it was time for

lunch. I was one of the first in the queue.

The lunch lady didn't look like she was

pleased to see me. (The lunch lady is

never pleased to see me – or anyone

else for that matter!)

I helped myself to a plate and looked into

the food bowls.

'Hello,' I said cheerily.

'Yes,' **growled** the lunch lady.

'I've been eating in your fine restaurant

20

for years now and I don't even know your name. Mine's Ted,' I smiled. She looked at me suspiciously.

'My name is Miss Monella,' she mumbled 'Sally Monella.'

'Your name is Sal Monella? And you are a lunch lady?' I asked. She nodded but didn't see the humour in it. Honestly, you couldn't make it up.

I just did. (Steven)
You can't speak, you are the author!
So?
So, stop talking to me and get on with the story.
Fine...

'Do you want food then?' she snapped.
'What's the choice?' I asked.

'Eat it or don't. That's the choice.'

'Oh, I'll have it then.' I said reluctantly.

Today was **brown goo with yellow bits** for main course and **yellow goo with brown bits** for dessert. I chose a table in the corner so I could sit on my own and think. Something had happened this morning and it had confused me.

Actually, it's more than confused me, it's left a **WEIRD FEELING** in my tummy. I don't know what to do about it, all I know is that it's a big thing in my life.

No, not big...

...HUGE...

No, not huge...

...MASSIVE...

No, not massive....

...hang on, let me get the thesaurus...now where is it? bear with me...oh, here we are...

balcony...
battleaxe...
beagle...
belt...
zebra (oops, too far)
Got it, big...

Great, large, important and difficult...
YES! All of the above

I needed to concentrate and work
something out. I should explain and maybe
you can help but, in order to do that we
need to rewind to the beginning of the day.
The trouble is I'm not sure how you spell
the noise that rewinding makes. Maybe it's
something like...

FRRRLLLLLLwwwLLLLPPPP

Or maybe...

BLLLLLLAAAALLALALALALLRRPPP

Or perhaps...

WLLLLFRLURPPPPPLLLL

No, definitely not that one, let's go with the first one.

OK, so let's rewind to the start of the school day. Ready...

FRRRLLLLLLWWWLLLLPPPP

The day didn't start off as well as I had hoped. Chloe Onions (the girl in my class who I am in **love** with) hadn't acknowledged me – if anything I was worried that she had been ignoring me lately. So, I was trying to get her attention without the teacher seeing. I'd tried to catch her eye by pulling **silly faces,** but she didn't notice, so I went a stage further and threw a pencil sharpener at her. Unfortunately, it hit her on the forehead and she started **crying.**

When the teacher asked who threw it, I didn't own up. (Yes, I know, throwing a pencil sharpener at the girl you love is not the right thing to do but I don't think any good would have come of owning up.)

Teacher: Who threw this pencil sharpener at Chloe's head?

Me: Me, Miss.

Teacher: Why would you do that?

Me: Because I love her.

Teacher: Oh, that's all right then. Off you two go and get married.

IT'S NOT GOING TO HAPPEN!

I would catch up with her later and comfort her and she will talk to me again. It's weird because I thought Chloe and I *were* getting on really well lately and then suddenly she **ignores me.** Why would she do that? What have I done? Maybe her best friend, Sandra Wum (AKA **Sandy Bum**), has finally convinced her that I am a terrible person – when in fact, Sandy Bum is a terrible person for not standing aside and letting Chloe and I become best friends. Anyway, all that is not the important bit. Stand by, the important bit is coming up... wait for it... here it is!

THE IMPORTANT BIT

Our teacher, Miss Simon, was calling the register when the door went. (Not literally, it didn't just sprout a pair of legs and walk off down the corridor. Now you've made me think of doors with legs and you've reduced the importance of the important bit, so we need to show how important it is by starting the important bit again. Because it's important.)

THE IMPORTANT BIT (AGAIN)

Our teacher, Miss Simon, was calling the register when there was a **knock** on the door and in walked Mr Munford, the head teacher, closely followed by a boy and a girl.

Mr Munford waited for us all to be quiet and then made an announcement. 'Morning, class. Welcome back everyone to this new term. I hope you are feeling **refreshed** and ready to learn. A new term means new people and **new friendships**. I'd like you all to meet Faith and Ed, they will be joining your class. Please make them feel welcome. Thank you.' He turned and left the room leaving the two new pupils looking slightly embarrassed. Miss Simon welcomed them with a smile and told them to go and find a place to sit. I looked around and noticed the two spare seats were either side of me. And that's where the problems started.

I turned to Ed.

'Hi,' I said, trying to make him feel welcome.

He nodded. 'I'm Ed, Ed Jones.'

WAITANDAWHOANDAWHATNOW?!?!

'Did you say Ed Jones?'

'Yep, I'm Ed, Ed Jones, what's your name?'

He can't be Ed Jones when I am Ted Jones!!!

How can he be Ed Jones? That's not allowed. Is it? You can't have a classroom with a Ted Jones *and* an Ed Jones.

It upsets the natural order of things. A black hole might open up in the middle of the classroom and swallow us all!

IT'S JUST ALL KINDS OF WRONG!

Besides, I only changed my name to Ted because it was the shortest name I could think of and now here's someone with my name – only shorter! He has the name I should have. The name I should've thought of. That. Is. Not. On.

'My name...' I said hesitantly. 'My name... is Terry Barry Larry Gary Harry Jerry Perry Lenny Benny Johnny Tommy Julie Jones.'

'Wow, that's a long name!' he said. 'Do people call you something for short?'

'For short? How do you mean?'

'You know, like a nickname or something,' he asked.

'Ummm...not that I... Ummm... I don't think so...'

'Ted Jones!' bellowed Miss Simon. I groaned. Ed looked at me, confused. I looked away. 'Save the conversations and introductions for the playground. We have a lot of work to get through.'

I avoided eye contact with ED (THE

NAME STEALER). I needed to think what to do about that situation when another situation occurred and that was an EVEN **BIGGER** SITUATION than the previous situation and – I think you've gathered by the name – that as far as situations go, the previous situation was a pretty big one!

You won't believe this but I'll try and explain.

CHAPTER 3

This is what happened...

I carried on with my work quietly, but secretly seething, when a scrunched-up paper ball bounced off my head. I looked around to see who had thrown it, but everyone was getting on with their work. I opened the ball carefully so as not to let Miss Simon hear me. Written on the piece of paper was a message. It read:

Hey! I'm Faith.

I looked around... who is Faith? Wait a minute! Is that the new girl? I looked to my left and looking at me was the new girl. She saw me notice her and smiled before crossing her eyes and sticking her tongue out, which made me **LAUGH OUT LOUD.**

'It everything all right?' snapped Miss Simon.

'Yes, Miss. Just something in my throat,' I replied before faking a cough and getting back to work. I picked up the piece of paper and wrote underneath her message.

Hi Faith, I'm Ted Jones.

I scrunched the paper back into a ball and carefully threw it to the desk next to me. I watched as *Faith* read it and gave me a little wave.

Well she was **nice and friendly,** wasn't she?

The ball of paper came flying back and landed on my desk. I opened it up.

Nice to meet you, Ted Jones. Isn't the new boy called Ed Jones? That's super weird. Anyway, I don't know anyone at this school so can you be my guide please?

Faith Brook

Now wait a second! Did you notice the same thing I noticed? Her name is Faith Brook. FAITH BROOK.

As in **FAITHBROOK**.

Who on Earth calls their child Faithbrook? (I know, I can talk, I have a ridiculous name but come on... Faith. Brook?!) I wrote another message back to her.

33

Your name is Faith Brook.
As in Faithbrook?!?
Like Facebook only FaithBrook?
Is your dad's name HughTube?

(I know, on the scale of funny jokes I just hit 10.5, right?)

I scrunched it up, threw it back and watched as she opened it. She laughed and rolled her eyes (not literally, she didn't pop out her eyes and roll them around, that would be silly). I watched her out of the corner of my eye as she wrote another message and flipped it back to me. As I grabbed it, Sandra Wum, who thinks she is the school police officer, raised her hand.

'Miss, Miss. Ted is writing, like, **secret** messages and, like, throwing them about.'

'Ted Jones, bring the message here.'

I groaned inwardly as I stood up.

(**Sandy Bum** is the worst person in the world ever). I handed a piece of paper to the teacher who snatched it out of my hand and looked at it.

'Why are you passing pieces of paper with **MATHS EQUATIONS** on?'

'Erm, because Faith wanted some help and I thought I'd help her as she's new. I was just being nice to the new girl, Miss.'

'Ted fancies the new girl!' shouted Martin Harris, the school bully. 'They are going to get married and do maths equations together. I've got a sum:

Faith + Ted = bluuuuurrrghh!'

he shouted, pretending to be sick.

The class laughed (because when Martin Harris says something you have to laugh or he'll **THUMP** you). 'Yes, thank you, Martin.

Maybe you could take a lesson from Ted and be a little **nicer** to people. Thank you, Ted, back to your seat but no more notes, Faith. If you need help, please raise your hand and ask me, not Ted.'

'Yes, Miss. Sorry, Miss,' Faith replied.

I walked back to my desk and as I passed Sandra, I stuck out my tongue. She immediately raised her hand to tell on me but I shot her a 'LOOK' and she lowered her hand again.

I'd managed to switch the paper for my sheet that had my working out on, pretty clever, huh? Everything was going remarkably well.

I looked over at Faith and WINKED. She smiled and silently mouthed the words 'Thank you'. Seconds later another piece of paper landed on my desk.

Thanks for not getting me into trouble, Ted. Seeing as I don't know anyone here and you are being nice to me, I'll let you sit with me at lunch time if you like? Faith x

I looked over at her. She was smiling. It lit up her face, she was very pretty. I gave her a thumbs-up to say that I would very much like to sit with her at lunchtime. Well, today was going well wasn't it? (Except it wasn't.) Because when I caught Chloe's eye, she was staring at Faith and then at me and she DIDN'T LOOK VERY HAPPY AT ALL.

CHAPTER 4

'I think I may have upset *Chloe*,' I told Ollie.

'Well, if you want to talk, I'm right here for you, Ted,' he reassured me.

'Thanks mate. Are you particularly good at relationship advice?' I asked.

'Nope. Not at all. I just like to be kept up to date with all the **gossip.**'

Well, at least he was honest.

'Why do you think she's ANNOYED with you?' Ollie asked.

'She hasn't spoken to me much.'

'She hasn't spoken to you much since **nursery** to be honest.'

'That's not true, we were getting on really well.'

'Well... if you say so.'

'I do.'

'So why don't you ask her what's wrong?'

'Are you *CRAZY?!* You don't just **ASK** someone what's wrong. What if they tell you and it's your fault?'

'Then you fix it.'

'What if you can't?'

'Then buy a new one online. Second-hand ones are often cheaper on auction sites.'

'Are we still talking about me and Chloe?'

'I'm not,' shrugged Ollie, flicking through a computer magazine.

(As I said before, at least he was honest.)

39

I don't like awkward situations. I'm a lot like an ostrich where that's concerned. When an ostrich feels nervous or in danger, it digs a hole with its feet, sticks its head in the hole and waits for the problem to pass. Although this is a great way of avoiding any kind of confrontation, it does show why the ostrich has never won a hide-and-seek competition. I like the idea of digging a hole and sticking my head in it whilst I WAIT FOR THE PROBLEM TO GO AWAY. Although it's not always guaranteed to work...

THINGS THAT WILL GO AWAY
IF YOU PUT YOUR HEAD IN A HOLE
(AND WAIT LONG ENOUGH.)

Air

Spiders

Laundry

THINGS THAT **WILL NOT** GO AWAY

IF YOU PUT YOUR HEAD IN A HOLE

(NO MATTER HOW LONG YOU WAIT.)

Homework

School dinners

Feelings

Sandy Wum

Suddenly, Ollie brought me out of my daydream. 'Have you signed up for the school play yet?'

'Nope. I can't act and I know nothing about 𝕾𝖍𝖆𝖐𝖊𝖘𝖕𝖊𝖆𝖗𝖊,' I said.

'Time to learn, buddy, because Chloe and Faith have both put themselves forward for the lead role of *Juliet* and, if you get the role of *Romeo,* then you know what that means don't you?'

'What?'

41

'Kissy-kissy time!' he made a kissy face, which was both unnecessary and disturbing.

I ignored his KISSY face but I was intrigued about where he got his information. 'How do you know that they have both put themselves forward?'

'I told you, I like to keep up-to-date with all the gossip.'

It made me think. If I got the role of Romeo, and Chloe was Juliet, then I would spend tons of time with Chloe and that was a GOOD THING. But what if Faith got the role of Juliet? Then I'd spend tons of time with Faith and that would be a GOOD THING too... but also maybe a **BAD THING.**

I don't know what to do!

(Quick! Fill out this questionnaire and send it back to me.)

WHAT SHOULD TED DO?

Try to get the role of *Romeo* ☑

Don't try to get the role of *Romeo* ☒

Dig a hole and stick his head in it ☒

(Thanks, there will be a short pause while I count the votes.)

...

'TED JONES! I've been looking for you.'

'Yes, Sir.' Came the reply but it wasn't from my mouth. (Nor was it from any other part of my body – I'm not that talented!) It was from ~~TED~~ Jones.

43

'Not you, Ed, I'm talking to Ted,' said Mr Munford.

I gave ƐD a sly smirk.

'I took the liberty of adding your name to the auditions sheet for the school play. After your performance at the prom, I thought you'd be a great addition to the cast.'

'I'll put my name down too, Sir,' said ƐD. URGH! Well if he's going to do it then so will I. He's already stolen my name – he's not going to steal my part in the show!

Mr Munford stared at us and smiled. 'Good, good. I look forward to seeing you both there. Have a good day. MARTIN! PUT CHRISTOPHER'S DESSERT BACK ON HIS PLATE THIS INSTANT!' and off he marched.

So, it had been decided. I was going to

audition. I figured I was going to have to give myself a little advantage and start by going to the **toilet.***

*For your information, I didn't need to go to the toilet. Well, OK, I **did** but it's irrelevant. If my stories just involved me setting up for an **_INCREDIBLE ADVENTURE_** and then just going for a **wee** or a **poo** then I don't think you'd be very interested (and if you were, then that's super weird of you). Plus, my books would be called 'Ted and His Toilet', which (if the toilet didn't do anything except be a toilet) would have fairly limited opportunities for an adventure.

TED & HIS TOILET
Book 1

CHAPTER 1

Today I wanted to go **BACK IN TIME** and see what dinosaurs were really like so I rushed to the toilet and did a poo.

The end

(See, not a very exciting adventure!)

Fortunately, I have a toilet that enables me to **TRAVEL BACK IN TIME** and, in order to win the lead role of *Romeo* in *Romeo & Juliet*, I need to go back and meet Mr William Shakespeare (well, I kind of figured that if anyone knows what it's about, it would be the person that wrote it). But first, I need to do a bit of research...

CHAPTER 5

When I got home from school, I **RUSHED** upstairs. Mum shouted just as I reached my bedroom.

'**TED!** How was school today?'

'Boring.'

'What did you do?'

'Nothing.'

By now my mum had reached the top of the stairs and was standing beside me.

'I love our time together catching up with everything,' she said sarcastically.

I sighed.

She clearly wanted to **chat** and wasn't going to give up until I'd told her *something* – ANYTHING would do.

'Well, I've put my name down for the school play and there are two new people in our class.'

'How lovely! What are their names?' she asked.

'The girl is *Faith* and the boy is *ED*.'

'Ed?' she replied. 'That's funny, we were going to call you Ed!'

'Wait! What? You were going to call me ED and instead you decided on **Terry Barry Larry Gary Harry Jerry Perry Lenny Benny Johnny Tommy Julie.**'

'Well, naming someone isn't easy.'

'Neither is signing your name when your

name is **Terry Barry Larry Gary Harry Jerry Perry Lenny Benny Johnny Tommy Julie!**'

Mum just laughed and changed the subject.

'So, tell me about the school play.'

'This year we are doing *Romeo & Juliet* and Mr Munford wants me to audition.'

'*Romeo & Juliet*,' beamed Mum. 'My favourite Shakespeare play. How *romantic!*' she sighed. 'I remember when your father was *romantic*, he used to take me in his arms and kiss—'

'MUM! I don't know where you are going with that story but you need to stop!'

Mum laughed. 'Oh, Ted, you have no idea. I remember this one time when he—'

'STOP! MUM, NO!

I'm going to **hurl**, it's too **disgusting**
BLEEEUUGHH!' I pretended to be sick
all over the place.

'Yes, very funny, clearly you are a
good actor.'

'Is there a scene in *Romeo & Juliet*
where *Romeo* throws up all over the
place?' I asked hopefully.

'No.'

'Well, then I might struggle.'

'There is a *big kissing scene*
though. Who is playing *Juliet*?'

Hmmm, good question from my mum. What
if it was *Chloe?* No problems there, I'd
be more than happy with a cheeky kiss. But,

what if it's *Faith?* I'd only just met her.
She seems to like me though, and I guess
I'd be happy if it were her too. Which is
awkward. Chloe would **NEVER** talk to me
EVER AGAIN.

(**RIGHT!** Who just said that she doesn't
speak to me much anyway?! Come on! Who
was it? If it was **YOU** then you must put
this book down and go and stand in the
corner and think about how words can be
very hurtful. Especially as she is probably
going to be my wife eventually. You won't
be laughing then will you? **Who just
said yes?** Right, you go and stand in the
corner too. Fine, stand in a different corner.
No, you aren't standing in a round room. You
are? All right then, find a room with corners
and then stand in one.)

OK, so what if neither *Chloe* nor *Faith* get the role? What if it's someone else? What if it's Sandra **'Sandy Bum'** Wum?? **AAAARRRGGGGHH! NOT A CHANCE!**

If I have to kiss her I will definitely add in an extra scene where I throw up all over the place. **BLEEEUUGHH!**

Anyway, I can't worry about that at the moment. I have to worry about getting the role of *Romeo* and then I can worry about who plays *Juliet*. I sat on my bed and turned my computer on. I typed in the password.

No, I am not telling you my password!

No, it is not Il@veChlo3. What a ridiculous guess. That's much too obvious...

(I quickly changed my password after realising it might be much too obvious.)

I typed in **Shakespeare.** There were over 200 million pages.

(I hope there aren't that many in the play, that sounds like a lot of lines to learn.)

After a brief look through, I couldn't help but notice that Shakespeare and I had quite a lot in common.

THINGS I LEARNED ABOUT

William Shakespeare

THAT MADE ME THINK THAT WE HAVE

QUITE A LOT IN COMMON:

We are both writers. He is widely regarded as the greatest English writer of all time, which is rude because I am from England and my writing is excellent and his plays don't have any toilet humour in them, so they can't be that great!

Actually, there is quite
a lot of toilet humour in
Shakespeare's plays (Steven)
Oh, OK, but I found a website with
all the rude jokes on and didn't
understand any of them, so I win.
Just because you didn't
understand them it doesn't
mean...
I win!
Fine...

- He wrote **COMEDY,** History
  and **TRAGEDY.**
  I write comedy (my hilarious jokes),
  history (my **TIME-TRAVELLING**
  adventures) and tragedy (my
  relationship with Chloe...)

- He INVENTED words.
  He actually INVENTED 1,700 words that are still in use today!
  These include: downstairs, leapfrog, schoolboy, unreal, gossip and freezing.
  Recently, I invented the word

  FRRRLLLLLLWWWLLLLPPPP

  (which in case you have forgotten is the sound that rewinding makes).

- He didn't write anything between 1592 and 1594.
  Neither did I!*

  *To be fair, he didn't write any plays during that time because of the outbreak of the PLAGUE, and I didn't write anything in that time because I wasn't born yet so, not exactly the same thing, but still...

- He had a **whole time period** named after him!

The Shakespearian Times

That's impressive to have an entire period in history named after a writer. We aren't in THE ROWLING TIMES or The Walliams Times. If there were a time named after me, I'd like **1515** (Hahaha! it's a joke! I like 15:15 — quarter past three — because it's home time.) Actually, we could be in **The Toilet Times,** although that does sound like a newspaper that you'd read on the toilet. I would definitely read **The Toilet Times** on the toilet (when I'm not standing in it!).

Well, that's a good start. Time to go and

meet the **great writer,** but I couldn't decide what year to **TRAVEL BACK** to. I checked my watch. **16:10**. Well, that's as good a time as any. My watch has decided I will go back to **1610.** Well done, watch.

I went into my bathroom, locked the door and took off my shoes and socks. (I don't actually need to take them off as, when I arrive back, I'm always completely dry but it just seems weird putting my foot into the water with them on. I mean, you don't swim in shoes and socks, do you?)

You do?

OK then, sure, that's fine, you go ahead and do that then. Good luck with that. Enjoy your swim.

So anyway, I took off my shoes and socks and stepped into the toilet. (Why don't they make toilets that have warm water in them?)

Note to self: Invent a half-jacuzzi half-toilet with warm, bubbly water. Aimed at people who like sitting on the edge of their toilet and dangling their feet in the bowl.

I don't think those people exist... (Reader) Fair point.

Actually, why would you ever need warm water in a toilet? The closest most people get is that tiny splash you get on your bottom when you do a really large poo. Even that isn't particularly annoying (the splashback, not the big poo).

Note to self: Do not invent a toilet that warms the water or a half-jacuzzi half-toilet. They are both silly.

So, I climbed in and flushed the chain,

reciting the date over and over in my head.
The water came up to my ankles as I started
to turn around and round. **FASTER** and
FASTER I spun. I took a huge breath
in and... **THHHWOOOOSHHH!** I was sucked
down the pan and round the u-bend. I
whizzed along the pipes picking up speed
at every turn. I felt my ears **pop** like on
a plane as I climbed and dropped faster
and faster through the pipes. The noise of
the water was deafening. I let out a little
WEEEEEEE! (Just so that you are clear, I
meant the sound, not that I actually let out a
little wee. Thank you.)

All of a sudden, I **STOPPED.** I caught my
breath. I had no idea what time I was in,
but I knew I hadn't arrived yet because...
well, because I hadn't arrived yet! I was
completely still. Waiting. I heard a rumble.

It got **louder** and **louder.** I turned to see all the water building up behind me. Eventually there was enough to force me onwards. I *SHOT FORWARDS* at terrific speed and performed eight loop-the-loops in a row. My stomach lurched and I felt sick and then I felt... nothing.

I was floating, like on a cloud.

There were no sounds at all.

I lay back, closed my eyes and relaxed. I must've dropped off to sleep because when I opened my eyes, I was in a strange room.

The floor was hard and dusty. I stood up and brushed the dust from my clothes. In the corner was a small, brown wooden desk and sitting in a big brown wooden chair was a big, brown wooden man...

I'M JOKING!!!

Sitting in the chair was a tall, thin man.

He had a small moustache and he looked almost bald from the front, except he had **wavy** hair at the back. (It wasn't a great look to be honest, but I wasn't going to say so.) He hadn't noticed me as he was deep in concentration. Every few moments, he dipped a large *feather* into a pot of **black ink** and continued to write with it on a piece of paper.

By the way, the feather is actually called a **quill**, and was a large goose feather with the end carefully cut to create a nib.

That's just weird, isn't it? Who was the first person to look at a goose and think, **'I could write with that!'**? How many animals did they attempt to write with before deciding on a goose?

Tiger:- too **BITEY**.

Elephant:- too **HEAVY**.

Hamster:- too **messy** (although good for colouring in large areas, I imagine).

Anyway, where was I? Oh, yes. I watched him for a little while then coughed into my hand to get his attention. 'Ahem.'

'Yes,' he said without looking up. 'I wondered when thou would speaketh.' He put his quill into a small container on his desk and turned slowly to face me. 'And who art thou?' he asked.

'Who art the what?' I was confused.

'Thou art What?'

'You what?'

'No, I am Shakespeare.'

'I am Jones.'

'Jones What? Thou dost hath a strange name. And what dost thou want?'

'Do you mean, "what do I want?"'

'Don't correct me! I am Shakespeare,
the greatest playwright
that England has ever known!' shouted
Shakespeare (the greatest playwright that
England had ever known). (Apparently.)

'OooOOooooh. Get thee!'

'Get thee what?' asked Shakespeare.

'Oh, don't start that nonsense again. Look,
I know words like "**thou**" and "**dost**" are
very *you* but they confuse me so perhaps
we can just stick to "you" and "do" and words
like that.'

'Very well, Jones. I will make things simple
for you. Listen very carefully.' He leaned
forwards on his chair and I leaned towards
him. He beckoned me to come closer
with a wave of his hand. I took a step
forward and leaned in even closer.

'**Go away,**' he whispered.

'Well, that's rude. I've come all this way to ask you a question.'

'Well, I'm busy!' he snapped. 'Writing plays. Because I, Shakespeare, am the greatest—'

'Yes, yes, I got it, the greatest playwright in England. My mum always told me that it's nice to be important, but it is more important to be nice.'

'Well, your mother is a poisonous bunch-backed toad,' sniffed William as he turned around and picked up his quill.

'Rude! Well, if I was a famous writer, I'd write with something better than a feather! Even if it has been specially carved. It's still silly.'

(OK, let's pause. I get that this meeting isn't going as well as I had first hoped and I am now having an argument with Shakespeare

64

– which in itself is weird – but I was expecting him to be a bit nicer and **not call my mother a toad** within five minutes of meeting him. I also admit that insulting his writing instrument was incredibly lame. However, it did seem to have an effect.)

'Hmmm,' Shakespeare sighed, sitting back in his chair and admiring the feather. 'I have experimented with writing with *graphite* but there is nothing so beautiful as the feel of a goose feather on paper.'

'What about the feeling of underwear fresh out of a *tumble dryer?*'

'I have no idea of what you speaketh,' said Shakespeare.

'Well, that makes two of uth!'

'Thou hast no manners. Thou art *RUDE.*'

'I hast lots of manners, actually, and thou arst rude,' I argued.

This was not a great start to our friendship. We had only known each other a few minutes and we'd already had two arguments. I needed to start this conversation again. And this time be really polite.

'Why do you say words like "**thou**" and "**art**" and "**hast**?" ' I asked, after an awkward silence.

'Because it is grammatically correct to do so. There are three ways of saying "*you*". When you are the **subject** of the sentence, it is **thou**, (thou art annoying me) and when you are the **object**, it is **thee** (I am being annoyed by thee). When there's a group of you, it's **ye**. Of course then there is **thy** and **thine**...'

'And thigh,' I interrupted.

'Thigh?'

'As in "would you like a **drumstick** or a thigh?"'

'What art thou talking about?'

'Chicken.'

'Why art thou talking about chicken?'

'I like chicken. Especially thighs. *"I have thy* **thighs** *for thine thupper"*... er... I mean supper."'

'Right, well, I don't think you've grasped proper language **at all.** Don't they teach ye young ones anything?'

'I art learning in art,' I said, trying my best.

'Doth *NOT* make sense,' he replied shaking his head slowly.

I tried harder, and threw in a few –*est* and –*eths* for good measure. 'I hast cometh to see-est **thou** becauseth **thine art** the *greatest writer* and **thy** plays art very good... etb.'

'Much better! But as you clearly can't speak properly and, let's be honest, the ENGLISH language is changing and more and more people are speaking like you.'

'Correctly?'

'No! Incorrectly. But anyway, I will make an effort so that we can understand each other. So, what exactly doth – sorry – do, you want from me?' asked Shakespeare.

'Nothing. I just want to watch a great—'

'THE greatest!'

'Sorry, the greatest writer in England at work.'

He smiled at my compliment.

I was winning him over. But I decided definitely not to mention that I wanted to be an actor until we were getting on much better.

CHAPTER 6

'I want to become an actor,'
I said, instantly forgetting what I'd said to
myself a few moments ago.

'An actor? You? And why do you want to
be an actor?'

'I want to get the lead role in a play, then I
will win the heart of my one true love.'

'Interesting. I do like a love story. I've
written many. ANTONY AND CLEOPATRA
– have you seen it?'

'No,' I said.

'Orsino and Viola in Twelfth Night – have you seen it?'

'No,' I said.

'What about Benedick and Beatrice in Much Ado About Nothing. Have you seen it?'

'No.'

'Hamlet and Ophelia. Have you—'

'No, no, no. I'm sorry, I've not seen any of them. I will, I promise especially Ham sandwich and big Delia.'

'Hamlet and Ophelia!'

'Yes, them. I will watch them. I promise. But right now I have to think about my own romance with Chloe and that means I need to become a really good actor. Can you help me? Please?'

'Hmmm. Interesting. I see a connection here as I too aspire to be an actor.'

'You do? But you are a *writer*.'

'And an actor. But no one respects me as an actor. It's rare that I get cast in my own plays. **Who better** to act the beautiful characters that I create **than I?**' William bellowed as he stood and waved his arm around in an elaborate gesture. 'Come, we must travel to the **GLOBE THEATRE** in London. We will each demand that we are given a part in this, my latest play.' He picked up a pile of paper and grabbed his cloak.

'Penelope picked up a pile of paper perfectly,' I said.

'Who?' he asked.

I had an idea. 'Try saying, "Penelope picked up a pile of paper perfectly", really fast.'

'Why?' asked Shakespeare.

'Because it's fun.'

'It doesn't sound much fun.'

'Try it,' I encouraged.

'NO,' he snapped, folding his arms and staring at me.

There was an uncomfortable silence.

'Well, OK then. Let's go. How do we get to LONDON?'

'If you are rich, you travel by horse; if you are *poor,* you walk. Are you RICH?'

I put my hand in my trouser pocket and pulled out a button, a pen top and two half-chewed sweets covered in pocket ꝼꞁuꝼꝼ.

'Erm. . .' I studied my pocket treasure. 'Based on my current status, I'd have to say . . . no.'

'Me neither. Although one day I will be. You mark my words! Until then, it's a hundred and two miles from Stratford to LONDON. It will only take us about six days to walk.'

'Six days! I can't walk for six days! I don't even have any shoes,' I whined looking down at my bare, dirty feet.

'Shoes? Shoes are for the RICH and we have established you have no money. No money. No shoes.'

'I can't walk barefoot for six days! Besides I have a very short attention span. I can't do anything for six days!' I argued.

'Nonsense, I have my finest ideas whilst walking. All we need is a strong sense of ADVENTURE and our imaginations. Who knows what will happen?'

'I'll tell you what will happen, Mr William Shakespeare, sir. I will get sore feet and I'll probably die before I get there!'

'Jones, you are very dramatic. That is good, you are on your way to becoming an

actor. Come, let us begin our *JOURNEY.*
This is a very good idea.'

This is a very bad idea, I thought.

I urgently needed a plan to save my poor feet. Here's what I came up with:

THE PLAN

- Start walking until I get tired.
- Pick the perfect moment to jump back home.
- Work out the date six days ahead from when we set off.
- Jump back and meet up with Shakespeare just as he finishes the journey.
- Award myself a large slice of cake for being so clever.
- Find cake now and then eat cake now rather than concentrate on plan.

I looked around **Shakespeare's** room but I couldn't find any cake. In fact, I couldn't find much where I was standing. There was a small wooden desk where Shakespeare was sitting on an uncomfortable-looking wooden chair, and just behind him was a large four-poster bed.

(Just to clarify I don't mean four big pictures of his favourite celebrity, I mean four posts that went up to the ceiling. Yes, I know that pictures of your favourite celebrity are also called posters but they are a different kind of poster. Look, I know it's confusing but I didn't invent the language, did I? Blame Shakespeare!)

On the posts, hung thick curtains.

'I like the fact that your bed is next to your desk. I would like a bed next to my desk at school.' I said.

If Shakespeare heard my comment, he

ignored it. He was busy gathering up his belongings. He packed an old, **worn-out** leather bag with a few clothes and then carefully wrapped his *quill* and *inkpot* before placing them in his luggage.

'I am ready for our **ADVENTURE,** young Master Jones. Let us set off while the sun still shines. We rest at MIDNIGHT.'

'I like to be in bed by ten otherwise Mum says I get moody.'

'If moody is what you are, then moody is what you shall be. We will nurture these emotions and make an actor of you yet. Come.' He ushered me out of the door and began walking briskly down the street.

'Slow down! I can't keep up this pace for *six days*.' Although at least I'd have time to ask him lots of questions.

'My only rule,' announced Shakespeare,

'is that, as we walk, you don't ask me any silly questions.'

'When do I learn how to be an actor then?' I asked.

'When the time is right, then you'll know,' he replied, waving a hand enigmatically.

'Please, Mr Shakespeare, I can't go on!' I was crawling on my hands and knees, gasping for air. 'I am tired, hungry and thirsty. How long have we been travelling?'

'Approximately three minutes. Now, get up and stop being silly. I can see your acting is getting better, though. Keep it up!'

We walked through the town and I noticed the smell. It was HORRIBLE. 'That's not you, is it?' I asked Shakespeare.

'Me?'

'That smell?'

'Of course, it's not me! I do not know

what it is like where you live, but here people empty their **chamber pots** out of their windows and the rain washes it away into the rivers. I admit it can get a little...
PUNGENT!'

'That's fine as long as by chamber pot you don't mean a pot that people **poop and wee** in?'

'Well of course I mean that,' he chuckled. 'Where else are they going to throw it? It is cold and privies are outside. Visiting them in the **cold weather** is unpleasant, so we use a chamber pot.'

'And then **throw it** out of the **window?**'

'Not the pot, of course. Just the contents.'

'You do know I'm walking without shoes on here! **Who knows** what I'm treading in? Actually, I do now know and it's very **DISTURBING!**'

Note to self: All time travelling from now on will be with shoes

'What if someone is walking below the window? They will think it's raining yellow rain and then a poop lands on their head.'

'Clearly, then, one must be *careful* when walking under windows!'

'Well, then, one is not going to walk under any windows if it's all the same to one,' I replied.

'Come, young Ted, enough of your moaning. Let us enter this inn where you can rest and enjoy a cold beverage and I can enjoy a few moments of peace!'

I followed him into the inn. We went in the inn, and when we were in the inn, I wanted to be out! It was hot and STUFFY and smelled funny. It was also dark and creepy and very busy.

I looked around. At one table sat a group of **noisy** men playing a game with dice. At another, a group of SCARY-LOOKING people leaned in and spoke quietly between themselves. They were shifty and kept looking about to make sure no one was listening to their conversation.

'Criminals,' said Shakespeare 'Best not catch their eye.'

I looked away quickly.

We strode up to the bar. The barman turned to William and asked what he would like. 'Two ales, please.' I didn't worry about the ale, because I'd learned that ale was like a mild beer that children also drank as, in those days, it didn't contain any alcohol. It was so popular in the 1500s that it was drunk at breakfast, lunch and dinner. Maybe because tea and coffee hadn't yet arrived in BRITAIN and a glass of water was out of the question due to **HEALTH RISKS.** Water was very polluted in those days (unsurprising due to everyone having a poo and then flinging it out their window).

Suddenly, Shakespeare turned to me.

'What's wrong?'

'Nothing,' I said

'You are pulling a strange face.'

'Am I? Oh. Well, I'm deciding if I should go to the **toilet.** I'm not expecting them to be very **NICE** so I was deciding if I should hold on.'

'Hold on? For *six days?*'

'Hmmm, maybe not. I can't decide. **To pee or not to pee?** That is the question.'

Shakespeare stared at me 'What did you just say?'

'I said, "Hmmm, maybe not".'

'No! After that!'

'I said, "Oh! I can't decide".'

'NO! AFTER THAT!'

'I said, "To pee or not to pee?".'

'Hmmm. "To pee or not to pee"... That *is* a good question. It has a good ring to it.'

'Yes, I though so too. Feel free to use it. Then maybe you can say your next play is written by **William Shakespeare** and **Terry Barry Larry Gary Harry Jerry Perry Lenny Benny Johnny Tommy Julie Jones.**'

'I don't think that is very likely.'

I shrugged and jumped down from my stool. I took my glass and was about to head across the busy room when I caught sight of a familiar face in the corner. What?! How is that possible?! Where had I seen him before? Hmmm... and what was he drinking?

WAIT A MINUTE!

(It's just a saying, no need to wait a full 60 seconds before carrying on.)

He was drinking a **BANANA MILKSHAKE!** It was the same boy I'd seen before on my travels.

As soon as he saw me, he grabbed his milkshake and started to **RUN.** I wasn't going to let him get away this time. I put my drink down and told William I'd be right back. I set off after him.

'WAIT!' I called. But he wasn't slowing down. **I SPED UP.**

(Cue a big, exciting chase scene. You can add your own music and pretend we ran down long corridors, across rooftops, grabbing ropes and swinging through windows and back-flipping onto ledges...!)

What actually happened is that he

tried to run through a locked door and *I ran straight into him* — which was a relief as I was really tired after all the walking we had already done so I was in no mood to chase him very far.

(Admittedly I hadn't walked that far but it was still exhausting. You try walking through streets of **poo!** Actually don't, it's **DISGUSTING.)**

It wasn't actually a very exciting or dramatic chase, but you can make up your own chase scene. Something like this...

EXCITING & DRAMATIC CHASE SCENE

I ran ....

Then they ran ....

Then we both did amazing, incredible, brave and

dangerous stunts like ....

And..

And also...

But not ....

It all ended in this dramatic bit: ....

....

Thanks for that. That was a great
ending to a chapter!

CHAPTER 7

I was now face-to-face with the boy, who still had a **MILKSHAKE** in his hand.

'I've seen you before. You're the milkshake boy! I saw you last term in **Henry VIII's** palace! Who are you?' I spluttered excitedly.

'Well, yes. I'm **JAYDEN**,' said Jayden.

We shook hands. 'Why are you here? No, wait. **HOW** are you here? How are you drinking something that's not even been **INVENTED** yet?'

'Well, I've never told anyone this before

but I can **TIME TRAVEL**,' he whispered.

'WHAT! HOW? I thought I was the only... I'm Ted with a Time-Travelling Toilet.'

'Hi, I'm JAYDEN with a TIME-TRAVELLING MILKSHAKE.'

'Well that doesn't work.'

'Yes, it does. I'm here, aren't I?'

'No, the **TIME TRAVELLING** works. But the alliteration doesn't.'

'The what?'

'The alliteration, the rhyme. Ted and his Time-Travelling Toilet works. All the Ts. Micky and his Marvellous Milkshake works.'

'Oh, that's good that is, I like that. You can call me JAY if it helps?'

'How does JAY and his time-travelling milkshake work any better than JAYDEN and his time-travelling milkshake? You need to sort that out. It will sounds better for your readers.'

'My what?'

'Your readers. You do write down all your **ADVENTURES** and create books don't you?'

'No, I'm not keen on writing. I prefer **snooker.**'

There was a pause. We were both silent. I really wasn't sure what to say to be honest. But then something seemed to dawn on him. **'Woah**, wait a minute now. Back up a bit. So you REALLY time travel using your **TOILET?'**

'Yes. I time travel via my **toilet.'**

'What?!?' he shrieked. 'You go swimming in your toilet and end up—'

'Who said anything about swimming?' I interrupted. 'I just climb in and—'

Now he interrupted. 'You *climb* into your

toilet? That is **DISGUSTING!**
EWW! And I shook your hand!' He wiped
his hand on his trousers.

'So what? You aren't going to catch
toilet,' I pointed out.

'Yes, but you might have **something** on
them.'

'I don't walk around covered in **poo
and wee** any more than you walk around
covered in **Banana milkshake.**'
I replied, noticing that since our chase he
was indeed covered in banana milkshake... I
didn't mention it.

'Hmmm, good point,' he said moving a little
closer and trying to **sniff** me.

'And you can stop trying to sniff me too!
Look, I didn't decide how I **TIME TRAVEL**. It's
not as if someone came to me and asked how
I'd like to be transported through time and

I chose a **toilet**, did I? It just happened. How did you discover you could time travel?'

'Well, one day I was enjoying a banana milkshake and it was really **THICK** and I was sucking really hard on the straw and I guess I just sucked too hard and went down the straw and **BACK IN TIME**. Which means that the only way you could have discovered that your toilet has time-travelling abilities was by climbing into the toilet. **Why** would you do that?'

'It's a long story and one that I wrote down and you can buy and read,' I said getting in a clever **ADVERT** for my books, which you can buy and read. (Did I mention that you can **buy** and read my **books**, you know, my **books** that are available to **buy** and read? Actually, by reading that, then you probably already know that you can read it because you were reading it when you read that.)

'Anyway, how are you always in the same place I am?'

'Coincidence,' he shrugged.

'It's not a coincidence. There are millions of possibilities. Years and years of history in any country. It's **not** a coincidence.'

'Yes, it is,' he argued.

'No, it isn't. Tell me the truth.'

'All right then. When I want to time travel, I just make myself an extra thick **Banana MILKSHaKe** and I suck the straw so hard I suck myself back in time. I just have to say where I want to go and I appear there. The problem is, I can't ever think of anywhere interesting to go so I just say wherever Ted goes and that's where I end up. Although I don't think much of this place. It smells awful!'

'I know. People poo in pots and throw it out of the window. But anyway, how do you know my name?' I asked.

'I read your books. I particularly liked the one about the EGYPTIANS.'

'What! What? I haven't been to Egypt!'

'Ahh, yes. I forgot to say. Sometimes the straw gets all creased and my time-travelling goes a bit loopy and sends me into the FUTURE. So, just letting you know, you do go to EGYPT. Cool, huh?'

'Sounds exciting.'

'It kind of makes your toilet sound a bit BASIC doesn't it?'

'NO! What's basic about a time-travelling toilet? It's a toilet that travels BACK IN TIME. How is that BASIC?'

'Well, **BASCIALLY** it can't travel into the **FUTURE,** can it?

'Whatever. So you have endless possibilities, travelling forwards and backwards in time. What have you seen?'

'The **snooker**.'

'That's it?'

'That's what I go for. I like snooker. In the future snooker is... well, the same really. Which is good because one thing about me is that I like my **snooker** to be exactly like snooker. No need to mess with it if you know what I mean?'

'Yes... no... maybe...'

I scratched my head.

There was an uncomfortable silence.

We both looked at our shoes.

'Do you think there are any more like US?' I asked.

'What? Boys?'

'No, not boys! I know that other boys exist! I'm talking about **TIME TRAVELLERS**.'

'Probably. I once met a girl who had time-travelling hair band.'

'You're making that up aren't you?'

'Yes,' he admitted, looking slightly embarrassed. 'But it would make a good book wouldn't it?'

'No.' I replied 'Sooo . . .' I said.

'Sooo . . .' he repeated.

'Are you going to keep following me?'

'Well, now that I've met you and told you I'm doing it, the novelty has worn off a bit, so... probably not, no. I'll just go back to watching **snooker**.'

'Right,' I said, pleased at the response and not knowing what else to say.

'Right,' he replied, probably thinking the

same thing.

'So...'

'So...'

I shrugged and held out my hand to shake.

He hesitated.

'It's clean,' I said.

He shook my hand. 'Bye then, Ted.'

'Yep. Bye. Jayden. I may well see you around.'

'Yeah, we should, like, hang out in the past and do stuff,' he said.

'Really? That's cool. We could be like SUPERHERO time-travellers who meet up in the past to solve crimes.'

'Yeah, maybe... I was thinking more along the lines of you want to play snooker and had no one to play with.'

'Well, OK, I'll bear that in mind. It's not as EXCITING though, is it?'

'It is if you like **snooker** and I—'

'Yes, I know, you really like snooker.'

'But your idea could work. I could help you out if you need someone to travel **BACK IN TIME** with.'

'OK, cool.' We swapped phone numbers and promised that if we ever needed each other we would call.

'Bye then, T e d,' he said, putting the straw between his lips and screwing his eyes tightly shut. I watched with interest to see what happened next. His cheeks **sucked** in and he immediately started to **fade**, then he shot off down the straw. It was strange, but no stranger than flushing yourself down a toilet!. And his was definitely a tastier way to time travel!

Note to self: Write a bestselling book called 'THE TASTIER WAY TO TIME TRAVEL' full of recipes from history. That is THE BEST IDEA I have EVER had! Even better than the time I designed the PLANT POT HAT™. When your plant dies, don't throw away the pot, simply put it on your head. Stylish and practical. Anyway, I think I may be getting off the point...

I need to get back to **William Shakespeare.**

CHAPTER 8

I went back and joined **William,** who was enjoying his ale. I took a sip and *gagged.* Ale was revolting.

'Mmmm, thanks for the drink.'

Shakespeare laughed out loud. 'Your acting is improving, young Jones. I can see that ale is not your drink of choice. I was *almost* convinced by that little performance. We will make an actor of you yet!'

As we sat, I asked **William** about the

rules of acting.

'That is a good question. In order to be a good actor, you must remember the four Ps.'

'I do them most nights. Especially if it's COLD in the house,' I replied a little too honestly.

Shakespeare stood up and began gesturing dramatically with his hands. 'The four Ps are thus:

Project yourself – Speak to the people at the back of the theatre, not the front, and then **everyone** will hear you.

Pretend – Become the character. If you believe you are them, the audience will also believe you.

Perform – Be bold, be fearless. Don't hold back. Think about what your CHARACTER would do, not what you would do.

And finally,

Practise – Wherever you are, go through your lines *over and over* again until you can say them without thinking.

'That is what you need to be a good actor.'

'That's it? That's all there is to being a really good **ACTOR?** Four things?' I asked hopefully.

'Well, that and you also need to be a naturally really good actor.'

'Oh. Right...'

'Come. While you dwell on my words, we shall continue to walk. We have far to travel.'

'OK, I'll remember the five **P**s.'

'There were only *four!*'

'Yes, but I need to **pee**, so that's the extra one. I'm just going to the... er... **privy** and then we can be off.'

I ran to the toilet and hid behind the door. The advice from **William** was great, but I'd had enough of walking! I'd take what I had learned so far and use that in my audition. If I got the role, I could always come back and get more tips.

I closed my eyes tightly, **HELD MY BREATH** for three seconds and then quickly raised my right arm and pumped it **up** and **down** really fast. I repeated the word 'home' over and over again.

(It's a good job I don't actually need a toilet to ride home as the toilets around here are NOT the sort I want to climb into, if you know what I mean!)

When I opened my eyes, I was back in my bathroom.

I put my socks back on and opened the door. Mum was standing right there.

'Oh, good! Come on, hurry out of there, I want to give the bathroom a good clean.' She was carrying a **huge** basket filled to the brim with brightly coloured bottles and brushes.

'That's a lot of cleaning products for a small bathroom,' I told her.

'Well, there are just so many different smells to choose from, I can't make up my mind.' (That's one thing about my mum, she can never make up her mind.)

I looked through the bottles, reading
aloud the different smells. 'Tropical Breeze,
Pine Forest, Summer Meadow, SWEATY
GYM SOCKS, Monkey Armpit, Bunny
Rabbit Parp...' Mum snatched the bottles
away from me.

'Don't be so silly,' she snapped. 'Bunny
rabbits only eat grass, hay and flowers. I
imagine their parps smell quite nice.' Mum
tutted loudly and told me to go and do my
HOMEWORK.

(Actually, when I typed this out
I made a mistake and wrote, 'Bunny
rabbits only eat grass, hats and
flowers. I like the idea of rabbits
only eating hats...)

BUNNY KING RESTAURANT

MENU FOR RABBITS (WHO ONLY EAT HATS)

Starter

Bowl(er) of Soup

Main Course

Beanies on Toast

Porkpie (obviously)

Dessert

Ice Cream with Summer Berets

Bandanna Split*

Drink

Baseball Cap-puccino

*I know a bandanna isn't technically a hat but then rabbits don't really eat hats so, whatever.

CHAPTER 9

The following day, I was waiting in the lunchtime queue chatting to *Faith*.

Huh? What?

Why are you smiling? What does that smile mean? Shut up! I am not in **love** with Faith. We are just friends. I DO NOT always hang around with her! She is the new girl and I'm just being nice. OK, can we move on?

Eventually, I got to the front of the line

and looked at the **FOOD** on offer. The **dinner lady** stared at me. 'Do you want lunch?' she **growled.**

'What's the choice?' I asked.

'Yes or no?' she snapped back.

'Err... yes then. What's **that?'** I asked, pointing to a pot of bubbling clear liquid.

'**TOMATO SOUP**...' the dinner lady replied giving it a stir. 'But I didn't have all the ingredients.'

'Which ingredients didn't you have?'

'Tomatoes.'

'So, what did you have?'

'Water... and **salt.'**

'So, that's just hot **salt water?'**

'**No**, it's tomato soup. See it says it there.' She tapped a small chalkboard on which someone had written 'Tomato Soup'. 'Do you want it or not?'

'Not,' I replied and moved on to rummage through the considerably safer choices of pre-packaged sandwiches. Then, Faith and I (Stop it! I mean it! Just friends, OK?) went and sat down next to Ollie.

'Hey,' I said.

'Hey,' he answered. 'Soup's good today,' he said, slurping the salty water from a spoon.

'I'll be back in a moment, I need the loo,' announced Faith as she put her tray down and ran off. I looked up and saw Chloe heading my way. She came straight over and sat down next to me. (Which was both good and very unusual.)

'Hi, Ted,' she smiled.

'Hi, Chloe,' I gave her my best, most handsome smile back.

'You've got food stuck in your

teeth,' she pointed out.

Seriously, why do I never look cool in front of Chloe?

'You and Faith seem... umm... friendly,' she said.

'Yep, we're friends.'

'You seem to be hanging around together a lot.' (OH, COME ON! Not Chloe as well.)

'Well, she's new and she doesn't know anyone so... not really that much.'

'It's just that WE'VE not hung out at all.'

'I didn't know we could,' I replied a little too quickly.

Chloe laughed. 'You're funny. It's just that I thought we had... a thing.'

'We do. Do we? What thing?'

'You know, spending time together.'

'The most we've spent together since Prom is 23 seconds.'

'That's very specific.'

'I timed it.'

'That's weird.'

'Now I've said it out loud, I agree. Still,
do you want to hang out with me?' I asked
hopefully.

'Sure, but, you know it's difficult with
Faith always being with you.'

Just at that moment, Sandra 'Sandy
Bum' Wum came over.

'We, like, have to go now,' she announced.

'Where?' asked Chloe.

'Anywhere, just, like, not here,' she said
and walked off.

'Anyway, I'll see you later, Ted,' Chloe
smiled and followed after Sandra.

I put my head on the table in despair.
Why does life always have to be so
complicated? What do I do now? Lose

Faith as a friend or lose my future wife as... well, my future wife? **Arrgghhh!**

'Now what?' Ollie smirked at my predicament.

'I don't know. It's **complicated**!' I sighed as *Faith* returned from the loo.

'What's complicated?' she asked, pulling over a chair and sitting down next to me. 'Anything I can help with?'

Ollie looked up and **grinned** at me. I shook my head to warn him not to say anything **stupid.**

'Are you two **going out**?' he asked (immediately saying something stupid).

'No, we're just friends,' we both said together.

I **blushed.**

Ridiculous – I know – but I couldn't help it. I didn't want to lose Chloe or Faith. What was

I to do? Perhaps I needed to take a break.

OK, **TIME OUT, EVERYONE! WE ARE HAVING A BREAK. GO TO THE TOILET** (your normal, ordinary, non time-travelling toilet), **GRAB A SNACK AND MEET ME BACK HERE IN A FEW MOMENTS.**

OK, I'll now answer some of your questions. If you have a question send it to **tedstoilet@mail.com**. OK, hit me. (Not literally. That wouldn't be nice.)

Your question: What would happen if you and I both climbed into the toilet at the same time?

My answer: The toilet would break.

Your question: But what if we held hands?

My answer: Eww gross. I don't even

know your name.

Your question: But what if we said the words and did the actions at the same time. Would we both travel back through time?

My answer: That is a good question. Unfortunately, we will never know the answer as I will never allow anyone to time travel with me. What if I lost them somewhere in history? I'd have to go to their parents and say, 'Oh, I'm sorry, the last time I saw your son/daughter was when we were holding hands standing in the toilet.' It's never going to happen. Time travelling is something I do alone.

Your question: I've heard that in Australia the toilet water flushes anticlockwise, but in Europe it goes clockwise. It's called the Coriolis effect and is due to Earth's gravitational pull. Also, in France, some of the toilets are outside in the street and in some countries the toilets are just holes in the ground and you have to squat over them, remembering to move your pants out of the way otherwise you poop straight into your pants, which is fine but then there was no need to pull them down in the first place, you may as well have just —

My answer: Woah there! Slow down, toilet geek! Why do you know all this? You really need to get a new hobby. Take up a sport or collect something (other than facts about toilets). Yes, I have a time-travelling toilet but what you need to understand is that the interesting bit in that phrase

is 'time-travelling' NOT 'toilet'.
Anyway, you didn't actually ask me
a question, so I'll have to guess
an answer for you. If toilets are
your thing then, after a quick
search online, I have found that
there are toilet museums in the
UK, USA, Korea, India and Russia.
Have a good time! I hope that has
answered your question... that you
didn't ask me.

BREAK OVER!

CHAPTER 10

After lunch, anyone who had put their name down to audition was allowed to go to the drama room. One by one, we were asked to go into the classroom next door and read a passage from *Romeo & Juliet*. While we waited, Mr Peters had us warming up by pretending to be TREES... again! He really liked trees. I put my branch up... sorry I mean hand up... and asked if we could do something else, like a COMEDY character perhaps. Mr Peters lowered his glasses to the end of his nose and stared at me.

'**Comedy?**' he repeated. 'We are *trees*. There is no such thing as a comedy tree. That's why you'll never see a comedy on television about a tree. Trees are serious. Life is serious. Trees are life.' He then pushed his glasses back up his nose, clapped his hands twice and shouted, 'Continue,' to the class.

Later that evening, I asked my mum if there has ever been a **COMEDY** on television about trees because she watches a lot of TV. She thought about it for a bit and then said, 'What about Last of The Summer Vine?' and then laughed for ages and ages. I had no idea what she was talking about. I think it's a joke for adults. So if you are an adult and you are reading this (and why not?), then enjoy that one. If, however you are a child then I'm sorry I haven't a clue what Mum's joke meant!

Anyway, back to the audition. My name was eventually called and I went to the classroom next door. There were two teachers in the room and they smiled when I entered.

'TED JONES?'

'That's me,' I said.

'Good. Feel free to read from the script but put in as much expression as you can, and good luck.'

I took a deep breath to calm my nerves and thought about what Shakespeare had told me. The 3 Ps, or were there 4? Or 5? Wait! Stop! RELAX! DON'T PANIC!

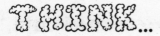 THINK...

There was:

Project – say it loud. Got that.

Pretend – really believe you are the character you're playing. OK.

Pyjamas – wear your pyjamas at all times. No wait! That's not it.

Perform – that's one of them. Be brave.

Passion – give the judges a big kiss.

EWW! No, that's definitely not one!

Pretty? Nope?

Parrot? Who's a pretty boy then?

Palaeontology – the study of fossils and dinosaurs? Why would I even think of that?

Pee – I really need to go to the toilet!

Practise – THAT'S IT! Practise!

I've done that. Right, here goes.

'Are you ready to begin?'

'Yes, I'm ready,' I replied. I took a deep breath, and let out a teeny, tiny, little parp!

(That's a secret, don't tell anyone!)
I began to recite the passage from *Romeo & Juliet*.

I pronounced every word as well as I could. I spoke as if I knew what I was talking about (I didn't a lot of the time, to be honest) and I projected as loudly and as clearly as I could. There was even a bit that I thought was sentimental so I lowered my voice and added an emotional wobble. I was acting – like an actor – doing the acting! I got to the end of the page and stopped. The two teachers clapped my performance and I took an elaborate bow.

'That was an EXCELLENT audition, Ted, well done.'

'Thank you. Did I get the part?' I asked hopefully.

'We have a lot of people to see,' the other

teacher replied.

'Well, you could just give me the part and we can let them go. There's no point in wasting their time.'

'Whilst I admire your confidence, I think it would be fair to at least let them *try*,' she smiled.

'Sure. OK, with me.' I shrugged and left the room feeling confident I'd done my best.

Surely, I'd done better than ED I'm-so-great-at-everything-and-I-go-around-stealing-people's-names-and-making-them-shorter JONES, and Stu if-you-put-me-on-stage-I'll-probably-just-poo-my-pants Hants. In fact, I don't even care if I don't get it (I do really) I just want to do better than those two. I'll have to wait until tomorrow to find out. I'll keep my fingers crossed.

CHAPTER 11

I got to school early the next morning and
ran through the gates. Mr Munford was
keeping watch as usual.

'No running in the playground!'
he bellowed.

'What about when we play football?' I
asked.

'Oh... Good point. Running in the
playground is permitted. In fact, it is
compulsory. Everyone, hurry up! **Start
running!'** he shouted at the pupils as

they made their way across the playground.

I ran down the corridor and **BURST** through the double doors leading to the drama department.

A crowd had gathered, all waiting for the names to be posted up. Suddenly, the drama teacher opened the door and poked his head out.

'I'm not ready yet, come back at lunchtime!' he said and shut the door again. Everyone groaned.

We all broke off and went to our morning classes, but no one could concentrate on anything other than who was going to be in the school play.

As soon as the lunchtime bell rang, we grabbed our things and **RAN** back to the drama room.

When I arrived, there was already a group

standing around the noticeboard laughing and talking loudly. I pushed my way through the crowd and read the first line.

Romeo..TED JONES

I GOT iT!

I was going to play *Romeo* in Stage Mount School's production of *Romeo & Juliet*. There it was in black and white. I was going to take the lead!

My eyes immediately dropped a line to see who had got the role of *Juliet*.

YOU WON'T BELIEVE THIS!

Taking the role of *Juliet*... in the Stage Mount School production of *Romeo & Juliet*...

Was...

... Ed Jones!!!!!

Haha! Only kidding!

It was actually Chloe.

So, there you go, the most famous

romantic couple in the whole of literary

history were going to play the parts

of *Romeo & Juliet*.

(Haha – again – I'm on a roll today it's

only 1:12pm and I'm already super funny.)

As I turned around to let other people

check the noticeboard, I was pushed aside

by **Martin Harris** as he shoulder-

barged his way through the crowd. He stuck

his face a few inches from the board and

stared for a few moments. Everyone was

quiet. No one dared move him out of the way.

'OH, WHAT?!' he shouted making

everyone jump. *'BACKGROUND?* I

don't want to be background!'

He made a sort of **growling** noise like a bear that's being annoyed by an angry wasp. Or a dog that's eating its dinner and puts its paw in its own water bowl. Or a... (Never mind, you get the idea!)

He caught my eye and headed straight over to me, pushing people aside.

'I'd make a better *Romeo* than you, Jones!' he yelled.

'But *Romeo* loved peace,' I said calmly.

'I like peas!'

'Not peas, *peace*.'

'Oh, that doesn't sound much like me. I like FIGHTING and ARGUING and **hitting** and that. OK then, who in the play liked... what's the opposite of peace?'

'Fighting and arguing and hitting...' I said.

'Yes, that. Who in the play liked fighting and arguing and hitting?'

'TYBALT,' I said.

Martin's eyes lit up 'Who's playing him?'

I checked the board. 'Stuart Hants.'

'Right then. **OI! Hants...!**' And off he stomped. I'm not convinced that's the *best* way of getting a role but, I wasn't about to argue with him, was I?

Suddenly, Ollie came running up to me, he was PUFFING and panting and nearly ran straight into me.

'I've got something **REALLY IMPORTANT** to tell you.'

'What is it?'

There was a pause. 'Oh. Annoying. I've completely forgotten!' Ollie pulled a face like he was straining in the toilet. 'Nope, it's GONE. I'll let you know when I remember.'

I went off to class shaking my head.

When the register was called and it got to

Chloe's name, there was silence.

Where was Chloe? She was in school this morning, I'm sure.

(I don't know why I'm asking you, you won't know. Wait! What? You do know? Where is she? She found a magical puppy and went into space. Oh really? Very funny.)

If you aren't going to be sensible then I'm not going to talk to you.

CHAPTER 12

I'm still not talking to you.

CHAPTER 13

Chloe was never off school. She was never SICK, ever. And if she was, I bet she would still come to school, even if it meant spreading her germs around – which would be fine, I'd be happy to have some germs if they were hers! Something was definitely wrong. I really wanted to know where Chloe was and if she was OK.

But first, lunch.

I needed to eat and think. The lunch lady was waiting with an evil smile on her face. I think I actually heard her **chuckle** as I approached her.

'What's on the menu today?' I asked **cheerily.**

'Meat.'

'What kind of—'

'**Substitute**. Meat substitute,' she interrupted, pointing to a bowl.

I peered into the bowl. 'But that's just carrots.'

'That's what I substituted the meat with.'

I was feeling brave – how bad can a plate of carrots be? 'Go on then, I'll have that please.'

'It comes with potatoes. Boiled or mashed?'

Again, I peered over the counter. 'I can only see boiled,' I said. She continued to stare at me as she raised her hand in the air.

She was holding a **ROLLING PIN.**

'Umm... Boiled is fine.'

She shrugged and put the rolling pin down.

I took my plate of carrots and potatoes over to an empty table and sat down.

Ted needed to think.

(I don't usually refer to myself in the third person. I did it to add drama to the moment.)

Ted added drama to the moment.

Ted continued with his story.

I shovelled a forkful of food into my mouth and made a decision. Actually I made two:

First decision – never eat school dinner potatoes again.

Second decision – to find out where Chloe was, I was going to have to do something that I'd promised myself I'd never ever do... speak to **Sandra Wum.**

I looked around the hall and saw her in the corner with a group of girls. She was talking and waving her arms around. I caught some of her conversation.

'It was, like, **SO BAD**, her ankle was, like, swollen to the size of, like, a watermelon!'

What? Could she be talking about *Chloe?* Her ankle is the size of a watermelon? That's OK. I would still marry her. I would just avoid looking too closely at her massive ankle.

I needed to find out for sure. Right, here goes. DEEP BREATH. It'll be fine. She's a human being. JUST!

I went over and stood beside her. She had finished talking to the other girls and was busy **TEXTING ON HER PHONE.**

'Hi, Sandra,' I smiled. She didn't look up.

'Hey, Sandra,' I said a bit louder.
She looked up at me. Tutted loudly, rolled her eyes and went back to **TEXTING**.

And you wonder why I don't like her.

You **DO** wonder? Then you really haven't been paying attention!

'So, I was wondering if you knew why Chloe wasn't in school?'

'Yeah,' she answered without looking up.

'And... So, can you tell me?'

She tutted loudly and stared at me.

'Why?'

'Because I'd like to know.'

'Why?' she replied.

'Because we are friends.'

'How nice. If you were, like, that close a friend then you'd, like, know, wouldn't you?' she sneered.

'Why?'

'Because, like, she'd tell you.'

'We don't have that kind of friendship. It's more **complicated** than that,' I said.

'You are, like, so weird,' she frowned.

'Why?'

'Because you are.'

'Why?'

'Stop saying why!'

'Why?'

'Look, I'll, like, tell you if you'll go away. She fell over in, like, netball practice and, like, **BROKE** her ankle. She's in hospital getting a cast put on.'

'Really! That's awful. Poor Chloe! Thanks, Sandy, you're a good friend,' I said sarcastically.

'Don't call me Sandy,' she snapped. 'Or **YOUR FRIEND!**' she shouted after me.

134

'**I** wouldn't call you if you were the only person in my phonebook!'

I didn't actually say that but I thought it. I just said, 'OK, whatever, **Sandy**,' and walked off. And she just rolled her eyes and went back to staring at her phone.

I had a big maths test after lunch, but I couldn't concentrate for thinking about 𝒞𝒽𝓁𝑜𝑒. What should I do? Should I go and see her? Should I buy her a present? Which hospital was she in?

Why am I asking you all these questions? And why don't you have the answer to any of them? Seriously, you aren't being much help to be honest.

I went back to my seat and ate a forkful of cold carrots. They tasted like soggy cardboard.

'Hey, Ted!' It was Ollie. He placed his dinner

tray down. It was piled high with food. Ollie loved school dinners. Ollie was strange that way.

'I'VE GOT SOMETHING TO TELL YOU!' We both said at exactly the same time.

'CHLOE'S IN HOSPITAL!' Again, at the same time.

'HOW DO YOU KNOW?'

This was getting weird. What if we were stuck like this FOREVER and could only ever say the same thing at the same time? That would be horrible. For a start, I'd have way too many school dinners.

If you consider that a really, really small, teeny, tiny number of school dinners was — in my opinion — way too much, then you get the idea that this wouldn't work out well for me.

'Sandy told me,' I said.

'You spoke to Sandra?'

'Yes.'

'**EWWW,**' he said pulling a face.

'How did *you* know?' I asked.

'My dad told me.'

'How does your **dad** know before me? No, wait. How does your dad know full stop?'

'Because he's a nurse.'

'He is? Really? You never told me he was a nurse. I don't think I've ever actually met him—'

'He works nights.' Ollie interrupted by way of an answer, which wasn't an answer at all!

'—I thought he was a ghost or a vampire or a knight.' I chuckled at my hilarious joke.

'I'm pretty sure **knights** don't work nights... Oh, I see what you did there!' He laughed a bit at my joke (though he could have laughed more in my opinion). 'I think we may be getting off the point,' he said.

'What was the point?'

'Chloe's in hospital.'

'Oh, right. Yes. Awful. I should go and see her. Except, I've never visited anyone in hospital. What do I say? Should I take a gift? How do I be all caring and stuff? I'm not very good at caring for the sick. I had a goldfish once and when it got sick my mum told me to flush it down the loo.'

'I don't think Chloe would like it if you did that to her.'

'I'm not going to flush Chloe down the toilet! I just need to know how to be more caring!'

'Look it up. Get your Google out.'

'I'm sorry? Who says "get your Google out"?'

'Me, I made it up. I think it will catch on.'

'With who?'

'People. Everyone. People who **Google**.'

'Everyone goes on Google but no one says "get your Google out".'

'Well, they should.'

'No, they shouldn't.'

Whilst I was not willing to **'Get my Google out,'** he did have a point. I would need to go online and look up what to do so that Chloe is really impressed at how nice I am and falls in love with me. I've heard adults say that they get through good times and bad times together and it makes them stronger. This is a bad time. We need to get through this together.

William Shakespeare will have to hold on for a bit. I need to develop the right amount of sympathy and I think I know just who I can ask. But first, I am going to have to get my Google out...

AARRRRRGH!
I DiD NoT
MEAN To
SAY THAT!

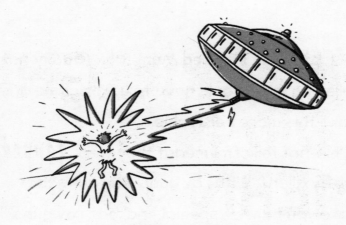

CHAPTER 14

When I got home, I immediately kicked off
my shoes and took off my coat, jumper,
T-shirt, trousers, socks and pants. I ran
upstairs. Realised I'd taken off too many
CLOTHES, ran downstairs, found my
socks, pants, trousers and T-shirt and
carried them upstairs. At that exact moment,
my mum came out of her bedroom.

'TED! Why are you running around the
house **NAKED**?'

'Umm... my clothes... err... just fell off.'

'**FELL** off?' asked Mum, obviously not believing me. I would have to up my game and make this more believable.

'No, not fell off. I meant they were *zapped* off. By aliens. With ray guns. Ray guns that make you naked... special... naked... ray guns...'

'Ted, darling. If aliens did decide to come to Earth, which I imagine would take a long time and be a very complicated, dangerous journey, I **DOUBT** the first thing they would do is find you and waste their time zapping your CLOTHES off.'

She had a point. It was rude but, she had a point. 'OK, well I didn't mean to take everything off. I just... forgot.'

'You forgot to keep your clothes on?'

'Yes.'

'I give up,' she shrugged her shoulders and left me to it.

142

I think that went pretty well to be honest. Anyway, I put my clothes on and turned on my computer. I knew exactly who to look up as we'd learned a bit about her last term. *Florence Nightingale*. This is what I found out:

FLORENCE NIGHTINGALE

1. She was born in 1820, and she decided she wanted to be a nurse in 1836 (wow, I still don't know what I want to be when I grow up and she decided her career when she was just 16 minutes old — Haha! it's a joke! It doesn't quite work but I'll leave it in anyway.)

2. She travelled to the Crimea (near the Black Sea, just up from Turkey) to help the injured soldiers there during the war and

discovered the hospitals were crowded, dirty and full of diseases — a bit like our classroom at school!

3. ...but seriously, she **CHANGED THE WORLD OF NURSING.** It went from being an menial, untrained job to a **HIGHLY RESPECTED CAREER.** And her insistence on cleanliness and sanitisation **SAVED HUNDREDS OF THOUSANDS OF LIVES.** Even today, every time we use hand sanitiser we can think of *Florence Nightingale* (as well as thinking 'ARRGGHH! I've got a papercut!')

4. She had a pet owl that she used to keep in her pocket.

5. She must've had very big pockets full of owl poo.

6. If she offered you a sweet from her

pocket, it would be a good idea to say no.

7. She wrote a book called **NOTES ON NURSING**, and some other ones with really long titles (see your local library for more details). I too wrote a book called Ted & His Time-Travelling Toilet (see your hands, right now, for more details).

8. She carried a lamp with her when she went round the hospital at night. That's why she became known as **The Lady with the Lamp**.

As I was searching, the doorbell rang. Mum answered the door and Ollie came running up the stairs and into my room.

'Hey, Ted. Have you learned how to impress Chloe with your caring yet?'

'Yes, look,' and I punched him on the arm. 'OWW!'

'I looked up *Florence Nightingale*.'

'Oh, I remember her. She was The Lady with the Limp.'

'Lamp.'

'No, I think you'll find she was known as the Lady with the Limp.'

'It's **LAMP!** She had an oil lamp that she carried around with her. It was a time before electricity.'

'Maybe it was dark and she walked into something. That's why she had a limp.'

'She didn't have a limp,' I sighed.

'I'll get my **Google** out if you like?' he offered.

'That's NOT a thing.'

'But it could be...'

'Let's hope not. Right, I need to go to the toilet, you can **get your Google out!'**

Please note: I actually did need to use the

146

toilet at this point. I mean, I am a normal boy and do sometimes use the toilet for normal things. I just don't write about it. (Except just then).

When I got back, we messed around for an hour or so and then Ollie and I went and told Mum about Chloe. She suggested she should have a nice cup of tea and an EARLY NIGHT, which is why I never take any medical advice from my mum.

Right, that's enough information. Time to meet the *Lady with the Lamp* and find out the best way of looking after Chloe. I will say and do all the right things and listen when I'm supposed to and nod my head *sympathetically* and she will remember how perfect I was and bring it up in her wedding speech, when we get married. Seeing as *Florence* had a lamp, maybe I should I take a torch with me? One day I might be known as the THE BOY WITH A TORCH. Actually, I'd be pretty annoyed if that were the case. I mean, I can **TIME TRAVEL** via my toilet, and if the only thing that people remember is that I once had a TORCH then that's missing out a big part of who I am and what I'm all about. (It's not even a very good torch.)

I left the torch with Ollie, who immediately started making shadow puppets on the wall, and I headed for the toilet.

I locked the door and climbed into the bowl. I repeated the date 1854, the year *Florence* travelled to Crimea. That should be about right. I closed my eyes, repeated the date over and over and flushed the chain. I started to spin, slowly at first, one turn, two turns. I felt the suction on my legs starting to pull me down. I spun one more time and then...

and then...

and then...

NOTHING!

CHAPTER 15

I was stuck!

Yes, stuck. In the toilet!

Actually, stuck! With the top half of my body sticking out of the toilet and the bottom half of my body already on its way to who-knows-where!

This had never happened before.

DON'T PANIC.

STAY CALM!

Things could be worse...

(Worse than half my body sticking out of the

toilet? I don't think so!)

I was just about to start panicking when I heard a **KNOCK ON THE DOOR.**

'Ted, love? It's your mum.' She didn't need to tell me that, but still...

'I forgot to tell you. Don't flush the loo. I think it's broken. I've called a plumber. But until he gets here, please don't do **number twos,** only number ones.'

'Right.' I called back

'Ted, love. It's your mum again.'

'Yes, Mum, **I know it's still you!**

'You **HAVEN'T** done a number two, have you?'

'No, Mum. I have not done a number two!'

'Good, the plumber will be here soon.'

'OK, Mum. No problem.'

BIG PROBLEM!

HUGE PROBLEM!
REALLY, REALLY
MASSIVE, HUGE, GREAT,
BIG ENORMOUS PROBLEM!

What was I going to do? A plumber was on the way to unblock the toilet. I could see what was going to happen:

Plumber: Yes, Mrs Jones. I can see the problem. Your toilet has been blocked by your son.

Mum: *TUT* Did he do a number two? I told him not to!

Plumber: No, no. It's actually blocked BY your son. He is stuck in the toilet. I'll get my plunger…

ARRGGGHHHH! What am I going
to do? Think quickly!

I wriggled and twisted and flapped and flipped and tried to get my arm free but all I managed to do was splash toilet water into my mouth!

(For the record, toilet water tastes exactly as you imagine it does. Really toilety. Why do cats drink from the toilet? Actually, since cats eat mice – and lick their own bums – I think toilet water is probably quite nice by comparison.)

Ugh! I spat the water from my mouth. Suddenly there was another KNOCK at the door.

'Ted, love. It's your mum.'

'YES! I KNOW WHO YOU ARE!'

'Are you all right in there? I heard some strange noises.'

'Yes, I'm fine, just, umm... cleaning my teeth.'

'It's 4 o'clock in the afternoon, why are you cleaning your teeth?'

'You can never have teeth that are too clean, can you, Mum?'

'OK, I guess not. Anyway, no pooing in there until the plumber's been.'

'OK, Mum, **I won't poo!**'

'Not until the plumber's been.'

'OK, Got it.'

'Then you can poo.'

'MUM! Please stop saying **"poo"**!'

'...**poo**...' she whispered and then giggled. I heard her footsteps go down the stairs.

Right, time to try again. This time with my mouth closed!

I wriggled and *wiggled*, jostled and *jiggled*, shimmied and **SHOOK** until eventually I had a hand

and an arm free. I stretched up and grabbed the handle and pulled it over and over.

I felt the water sloshing about underneath me. I was just about to try again when...

WHOOOSSHH!

...I was sucked down the bowl. **YES!** I'd created enough suction to send me on my way down the u-bend.

Out of the corner of my eye I caught sight of **THE THING** that was causing the blockage in our toilet. I'm not going to tell you what it was but let's just say that **someone** wasn't following Mum's rule. **And it wasn't me!**

I sped down the pipes, twisting left and right, up and down, over and under. Soon the pipes **VANISHED** and I was floating, through nothing, just peace and quiet. Soft lights floated in and out of my vision.

I breathed a sigh of relief and closed my eyes and waited to arrive.

Before long, I could feel that I was lying on a cold, hard floor. I could hear **coughing** and 𝔤𝔯𝔬𝔞𝔫𝔦𝔫𝔤. When I opened my eyes again, I was startled to see a concerned face of a young woman looking down at me. She had mid-length brown hair tied up at the back leaving a centre parting. She wore a *lacy bonnet* and a long black dress. She had two eyes, a nose in the middle of her face and below that a mouth...

OK, we get the point, thank you! (Reader)

Her face was ILLUMINATED by the yellow glow of a lamp.

'Oh you poor dear,' she sighed, her face full of concern. 'You look awful. Stay there, don't try to get up. I will fetch you some water and some medicine. Try not to worry.'

'Wait! What? I'm OK.' I protested.

'Yes, yes, I'm sure. You are being so brave.'

'Not really, I'm scared of cauliflower.'*

*This might need explaining.

Oh right, you want me to explain it. OK then. I once went to eat a piece of raw cauliflower and inside the bushy bit was a little silver bug. Since that day, I believe that living in the bushy bit of all cauliflowers are entire cities of tiny bugs plotting to take over the world. No one should eat cauliflower! Unless you LIKE the taste of cauliflower (and the taste of bug cities!).

Anyway, back to 1854. It seemed that time travelling and **panicking** at being stuck down the toilet had left me looking a bit... rough.

'You poor, poor boy. You are so pale and sickly looking.'

That's just rude, I thought. I was about to explain that sitting in my room playing video games can leave me a bit pasty-looking but I remembered that video games weren't invented until 1958.

(One of the early games was called Pong. It was an addictive game based on tennis and it was called Pong because after playing it for a few hours that's what you did – PONG – really badly.) (The last bit isn't true.) By today's standards, I bet the game was absolute pants. (Not literally, you couldn't actually wear the game – or any game – as underwear. Although with scissors and a large amount of sticky tape I bet you could make a nice pair of shorts out of a Monopoly board.)*

*I haven't actually tried this.

Anyway, back to 1854 (again).

'I'm OK, really,' I said. 'I don't need any medicine at the moment. I just need... to talk.'

'Talk?'

'Yes. It will make me feel much better if you could spend a few minutes talking to me.'

'Very well. A lot of patients just need to talk.' She smiled. Her smile lit up her face (or it might've been the lamp – not sure).

'What would you like to talk about?' she asked.

'You. How do you get to be so caring?'

She smiled again. 'I see this as an

opportunity to make things better. I am very lucky. Many girls my age don't go to school. It's sad that people think girls don't need an education. My family is WEALTHY and my father is a great man who believes **girls should be educated** and so he taught me at home. I've been given a rare opportunity and I don't intend to waste it. As my father helped me, I will help other people. Soldiers are brave men but the conditions of the hospitals are awful. Did you know that more men die of disease than fighting? If we trained nurses to cure the diseases and keep the hospitals clean, then fewer soldiers would die.'

'I had no idea,' I replied, transfixed by her soft voice. 'Can I ask you a question?'

'Of course,' she smiled.

'Someone special to me has had an

accident in and I want to visit them, but I don't know what to say. I've never been in a hospital before... until now.'

'Well, hospitals are cr0wᵈed and dirty and full of disease. Maybe one day they will be clean and safe places. You **MUSTN'T** just turn up to visit someone.'

'Oh, right. Yes, sorry... I mean they *were* in hospital but now they are back home, getting better. I'm still not sure what to say to them though.'

'Ah. Well, the most important thing to do is to *listen* to what they have to say.'

'Pardon?'

'I said the most important thing to do is to *listen* to what people say.'

'Oh, yes. Sorry. Quite right... I wasn't... anyway, carry on.'

'Hospitals can be **SCARY** and the

reason they are in hospital could be just as awful. There is a war going on, as you know. Terrible things happen in wars.'

'Yes,' I said, not really knowing much beyond what we'd learned in school.

'So, they will be **frightened** and lonely, but having someone to talk to can make them feel better while the doctors and nurses do their best to help them. Be there for them, comfort them and just listen to what they have to say.'

'I see,' I nodded. 'So that is the key.'

'No, that is the key,' she pointed to a key on the window ledge behind me. 'Would you mind passing it to me? It's important.'

I reached behind me and passed her a large metal key. 'Is it a magical key that unlocks a portal to another dimension?'

'Pardon? No, it opens the window. It can

get pretty **smelly** in here.'

'Oh, right. Of course.' I said.

'I hope you get better quickly, young man.
This hospital is no place to be. As soon
as you feel better, you need to go home.
I've heard there has been an outbreak of
DYSENTERY.'

'Which sentery?'

'What?'

'You said an outbreak of dis-sentery.
How is it different from dat-sentery or de-
other-sentery?'

'Dysentery is a **DISEASE**, everyone
knows that. Clearly you are still feverish. Let
me go and get you some medicine.'

She hurried away, down a corridor,
taking her lamp with her and leaving me in
darkness. I had got the information I'd come
for. Time to go home.

BUT WAIT!

What if I **COULDN'T** go home? My toilet might still be blocked. I might be stuck here with all the diseases.

The 1800s was no place to hang about. I needed to take a chance and see what happened. I closed my eyes and pumped my arm up and down. When I opened them again, I was back...

BUT...

BIG BUT!

(Not mine! How dare you! Why would you say that I have a big butt? I don't mean Big Butt, I mean Big BUT!)

Anyway, the problem was I was still stuck in the toilet. I closed my eyes and squeezed and wriggled my entire body. Nothing. I was jammed. It was a good job no one needed the toilet right now.

'Ted, it's your mum. Hurry up in there. I need the toilet!'

WHYYYYYY? Why is nothing simple? What is my mum going to say when she opens the door and finds my head poking out of the toilet?

The door handle rattled as Mum tried to hurry me up. I struggled, wiggling my body as best I could. I let out a **YELP** as I managed to get an arm free.

'Ted, it's your mum.'

'I KNOW IT'S YOU, MUM! YOU DON'T HAVE TO KEEP TELLING ME IT'S YOU!'

'What are you doing in there? You're making some odd noises.'

'Umm. I have a **tummy ache.** Must be the school dinners again.'

'What did you have?'

'Lasagne – I think.'

'What do you mean, you "think". Did it look like lasagne?'

'Not really.'

'Well, did it taste like lasagne?'

'Definitely not!'

'Then how do you know it was lasagne?'

'I don't.'

'Right. Well, I need a wee and you are in the toilet.'

Mum did not know how right she was! I was literally IN the toilet. Arrgghh! Just then, I heard the doorbell go. My mum tutted and went downstairs.

What do I do now? How am I going to explain this?

I was just practising my new balancing act and I fell?

I was really hot and decided to go for a swim?

I saw something in the toilet and wanted to get a closer look?

I was thirsty and...

NO!

ARRRGGHH!

I started to **panic** and threw myself backwards and forwards. I shook myself left and right and tried to bounce up and down. I closed my eyes and gave one last **heave** with all my might. There was a popping noise, like a cork makes when it flies out of a wine bottle, and I flew across the bathroom.

I was home.

I was free.

I was safe.

I unlocked the door, walked out of the bathroom and straight into a man wearing blue overalls and carrying a TOOLBOX. Behind him stood my mother, who crossed her legs and shrugged her shoulders. Behind her, I could see Ollie who was still making shadow puppets on my bedroom wall with my TORCH.

'Right, let's get in there and take a look, shall we?' said the plumber, scratching his head with the tip of a screwdriver as he passed me.

'You didn't poo in there, did you?' whispered my mum.

'Mum, please. I did not poo in there!'

'More FIBRE,' said the plumber, sticking his head back around the bathroom door. 'Bowl of bran in the morning and a big glass of prune juice. Sorts me right out.'

I didn't answer him but peered nervously at the pile of TOOLS he had assembled around the toilet. I didn't like the look of them at all. Any wrong move and he could damage my toilet, meaning I'd never **TIME TRAVEL** again. My future was in the hands of a man who scratched his head with a screwdriver and drank **PRUNE JUICE** for breakfast!

I was DOOMED!

CHAPTER 16

I couldn't sit around **panicking** about the plumber. I needed to go and see Chloe and demonstrate how caring and kind I could be.

'Mum!' I shouted. 'Me and Ollie are going to see Chloe in hospital.'

'Ahh, you LiKE her, don't you?'

'Mum! Stop.'

'It's OK. Don't be shy, you can tell me. I'm here if you want to ask me any questions. When your father and I started dating he was quite the romantic. He used to—'

'MUM! ENOUGH! No one needs to hear that... ever!'

'Don't be silly. Your father was *very handsome* when he was young. We would hold hands and go for long walks together and...'

'Good idea.'

'What is?'

'Going for a long walk. I'm off to the hospital. I'll be back for dinner. Hopefully the toilet will be fixed by then.'

'Let's hope so. Be careful, and say hi to Chloe for me.' She laughed and chased me out of the house blowing kisses as I ran for the front door. Ollie grabbed his coat and followed me down the road.

'You are in love with Chloe, aren't you?' asked Ollie.

'Not you as well?' I groaned.

'Wait! You love me as well?'

'No, Ollie. I don't love you. I like Chloe, but it's complicated.'

'What is?' he asked.

'Well, you can't tell anyone this but, I think Faith likes me.'

'Oh, I already knew that,' he shrugged.

I stopped walking.

'How could you know that? No one knows that. I only found out an hour ago!'

'MIA told me.'

'Mia? How did Mia know?'

Ollie sighed loudly.

'Sandra told MIA, and MIA told me.'

'But... how did—'

'OK, I'll explain.

172

Faith told **MATTHEW**

and then **MATTHEW** told Tia...

Tia told Oona

Oona told SCARLETT

SCARLETT told *HARRY*

HARRY told Amelie

Amelie told Muhammed

Muhammed told Dillon

Dillon told **Emma**

Emma told Sophie

Sophie told the other Sophie

the other Sophie told KATY

(with a Y)

KATY (with a Y) told Katie

(with an i and an e)

Katie (with an i and an e) told Kasey

Kasey told Stuart

Stuart told MR MUNFORD

MR MUNFORD told **Mr Peters**

Mr Peters told the **lunch lady**

the **lunch lady** told Miss Simon

Miss Simon told **Ella**

Ella told JOSH

JOSH told Mollie

Mollie told MARCUS

MARCUS told ABDUL

ABDUL told OLIVIA

OLIVIA told ISABELLA

ISABELLA told Krishnan

Krishnan told **William**

William told Hannah

Hannah told **LUCAS**

LUCAS told **ABIGAIL**

ABIGAIL told DANNI

DANNI told *Barney*

Barney told **Dev**

Dev told **Sandra**

Sandra told MIA

And then MIA told me.

I stood there with my mouth open.
"WHAT!? Four of those people don't even go to our school! And why are there three teachers and a lunch lady on the list?'

'News travels fast,' Ollie shrugged again.

'You are telling me!'

'Yes, I'm telling you because MIA told me, Sandra told her, Dev told—'

'I got it! I got it! STOP! I didn't want anyone to know. What if Chloe finds out? She mustn't. Don't tell her.'

'OK, no problem. Your secret is safe with me... and 33 pupils, three teachers and a lunch lady.'

I groaned.

'Wait here.' I ran into a newsagent and bought a small box of chocolates for Chloe.

'Right, let's go.'

The walk to the hospital took just over 10 minutes. I asked in reception where Chloe was and they gave me directions to the correct ward. I walked in and immediately spotted her. Her leg was in PLASTER, she was staring at her phone and she looked tired. I went up to her and tapped her on the shoulder.

'Hey, Chloe,' I smiled.

'Ted! What are you doing here?' She smiled. 'Hi, Ollie.'

Ollie smiled awkwardly. 'I'm going to get a drink from the canteen. Do you guys want anything?' We both shook our heads. He shrugged and walked off in search of something to drink.

'Ollie and I came to see you. I bought you these,' I said and handed her the chocolates.

'That's so sweet of you. Thank you. It's so nice of you to visit me. How's school?' she asked.

'The same.'

'Any news? Any **gossip**?'

'No, none really. Nope. Nothing.'

Chloe smiled but looked disappointed. Suddenly I remembered what I'd learned from *Florence Nightingale*. I got up and began checking the surrounding area.

'What are you looking for?' asked Chloe.

'I'm just making sure everything is clean and safe for you.'

'OK, that's nice of you... but, I think I'm good.'

'Did you know that in 1854 more soldiers died from DISEASE than fighting?'

'I didn't,' she replied. 'But, I'm still not sure

how that affects me right now.'

'Let's hope it doesn't.' I nodded, and sat on the edge of her bed. 'Right, if you are feeling lonely or **frightened** then feel free to talk about it.'

'Well, I'm not lonely now because you and Ollie are here, and I wasn't frightened until you started searching for **diseased soldiers** in my bedside cabinet.'

'Yes, well... you can't be too careful, can you? Let's chat.'

OK, when I look back, it was a bit **WEIRD** of me, but I was nervous. I'm not sure if I've mentioned it but Chloe is very, **very beautiful** and this was the first opportunity I'd ever had to chat to her without **Sandra Wum** interrupting.

'Oh. Hi, Chloe. Why is he, like, here?' interrupted Sandra as she walked into the room and glared at me.

NOOOOOOOO!
WHHHHHHHHHYYYYYY DOES
THIS HAPPEN EVERY SINGLE
TIIIIIIIIMMMME????

'He came to visit me. We were just having a chat,' Chloe smiled.

'Boring. I have, like, **SO** much gossip to tell you in, like, **private**.' She turned and GLARED at me.

'It's OK. Ted can stay,' said Chloe.

'Yes, it's OK. I can stay,' I repeated looking directly at Sandra. She shrugged but remained silent. We were all really quiet. It was very awkward.

Eventually, Ollie returned.

'Hi, everyone. The canteen was closed and I couldn't find a vending machine so I didn't get a drink.'

179

'Right then,' I said. 'I guess I should help you find one then.'

'Umm, OK. That'd be good. Bye, Sandra. Bye, Chloe, hope you feel better soon.'

'Thanks, Ollie,' she replied.

'It was really nice to see you, *Chloe*,' I said.

'Whatever,' muttered Sandra under her breath.

'Not so nice seeing you, **Sandy**,' I said and walked out before she could reply.

Chloe called after me. 'Thanks for coming, T e d. It was really good of you.'

I waved and she waved back.

'Did that go well?' asked Ollie when we were outside the hospital?

'For about five minutes and then **Sandy Bum** spoiled everything.'

'Did you tell her about Faith?'

'No, of course I didn't tell her about *Faith*. Why would I tell her about *Faith*?'

'Dunno. It's the latest **gossip**, isn't it?' he shrugged.

I didn't say anything. I don't like being the latest gossip. Unless the gossip went like this:

Girl: Hey, have you heard the latest gossip?

Boy: No, tell me.

Girl: Ted has been voted the most awesome pupil in the school.

Boy: I always thought he was very cool but now it's official.

Girl: And I heard that Sandra Wum has left the school forever.

Boy: I heard she dropped her schoolbag and when she bent down to pick it up she parped so loudly that she exploded!

I think I've just written the best play ever. If nothing else, thinking about that has **cheered** me up. I shall stop thinking about my current problems and focus on going back to visit **William Shakespeare** and getting him to help me perform the best version of *Romeo & Juliet* ever!

CHAPTER 17

When I got home, Mum shouted out from the living room.

'How was Chloe?'

'Chloe who?' I asked, being deliberately annoying.

'Chloe, the girl you just went to see in hospital.'

'Oh, her. She's OK,' I called back. 'But her leg is in PLASTER and she won't be back at school for a little while.'

'Poor girl,' she sighed and went back to

watching television. 'THE TOILET'S WORKING!' she shouted.

Well it may be working as a toilet but does it still work as a method of **TIME TRAVELLING**? Because, if it only works as a normal toilet, I'm not going to be able to travel back to see Shakespeare – or anyone else for that matter. I was nervous. My heart was pounding. There were too many 'what if' questions **buzzing** around my head.

I took a deep breath. It was time to test the toilet.

I went in and **LOCKED** the door. It looked the same (the toilet, not the door!), which was a good thing. I took off my socks and shoes, climbed in and crossed my fingers for luck. I started to think back to where I left off with Shakespeare and where I needed to be. I flushed the toilet and waited...

It began spinning me around and around. **Yes, it was working!** There was a loud sucking noise and I was off down the toilet at super *HIGH SPEED*. I'm not sure what that plumber had done but things were happening really fast. I could barely catch my breath as I zig-zagged left and right through the pipes. I was going so fast I COULDN'T SEE ANYTHING. Everything was a blur. It was like travelling in a rocket (if the rocket had decided not to go into space and travel down my toilet instead). It usually takes about five minutes to get where I'm going, but within 60 seconds I had landed with a bump on a grassy hill.

I stood up. I was a bit wobbly and **dizzy** from the speed of my journey. I caught my breath and brushed myself down.

'Come along!' called William as he strode

over to help me up. 'We are only a short distance from the **GLOBE THEATRE** in $\rm LONDON$. 'An hour's brisk walk and we will be there. Come, come. Keep up.'

Remember, time is different when you travel back through it. He wouldn't have even known that I'd gone.

'Where have you been?' he asked.

Oh, OK. That's weird.

'I've just been... umm... talking to someone over there... How are you, Mr Shakes?' I said cheerily.

He looked at me and raised an eyebrow.

'Can I call you "Mr Shakes"?' I asked.

'NO, you most definitely cannot.'

'OK. What about Shakey?

'NO.'

'Willy?'

'ABSOLUTELY NOT!'

'Fine. I'll call you **Shakespeare**,' I replied, not wanting to argue. 'So, what more can you tell me about acting in one of your plays? Specifically, *Romeo & Juliet*?'

'Well, you can't expect to play a role successfully unless you fully understand the story. Are you familiar with the play?'

'Yes, yes, yes... errr...'

'I thought as much. Right,' he sighed. 'Allow me to explain the story to you. We will start at the very beginning.'

OK, PAUSE THIS STORY!!!

At this point, **William Shakespeare** began to tell me the entire story of *Romeo & Juliet* in great detail. I am not going to repeat everything that he said due to a combination of time and really complicated copyright laws. Instead, I give you a new version of *Romeo & Juliet*. But I will make it really easy to understand because I will use me, my life, and the people in my life. Great idea, huh?

Here we go...

Stand by... This is really happening.

(Apologies to fans of William Shakespeare and to William Shakespeare himself.)

Tedio and Chloliet

A beautiful love story and a tragedy, loosely based on Romeo & Juliet. Written by Tedeo

'Oh, hello, my name is Tedio, I live in Italy. Ooh! It is hot and I am eating spaghetti and pizza. Over there is the Leaning Tower of

Pisa and the Colosseum and isn't that the Trevi Fountain?'

OK, we get the point. You're in Italy. Move on. (Reader)

There is lots of arguing and fighting in our town. (In Shakespeare's play it was two families who were fighting. The families were called the CAPULETS - sounds like tablets you take when you have really BAD WIND - and the MONTAGUES - sounds like a posh neighbour who wears a hat and likes gardening. Instead, I will base it on my crowd - of which I am the leader - called the AWESOME SQUAD and Stuart Hants's stupid crowd called the POO CREW).

Both crowds hate each other and never talk to each other. I am in love with *Rosaline.* (*Romeo* was in love with Rosaline, and there's no Rosaline in my real life, but I didn't want to put, like, Faith here or anyone real

in case Chloe read it and got the wrong idea!)

Romeo's best friend was called BENVOLIO.

However, in this story, my best friend is called

BEN OLLIE-O and he tells me to forget about

Rosaline and instead come to a fancy-dress

party at Stuart Hants's house. This could be

really dangerous because Stuart Hants has

been known to poo his pants, and if we were

recognised then he would get angry and it

might happen again and it would totally ruin the

party. However, we decide to go.

At the party, I end up sneaking away and

talking to Chloliet and she is amazing and

I forget all about Rosaline and fall in love with

Chloliet. I tell her and guess what – she has

fallen in LOVE with me too! We agree

to meet up the next day in secret and get

married. (You'll have to imagine that A. we are

190

older and B. we really don't think things through properly.) Then, Stuart Hants finds out we were at his party and gets cross and wants to have a *FIGHT* but I don't want to have a fight because I don't like fighting and if we were rolling around fighting then Stu Hants might suddenly poo his pants (which he is known to do – see above). But everyone gets annoyed and everyone starts fighting until the headmaster steps in and breaks it all up but now he is very cross and **shouty** and red in the face and he asks whose fault it is. The Poo Crew blame me for starting it (which is totally wrong), and he decides to *expel* me from school, but I run away because if he can't find me, he can't officially expel me (remember, I don't really think things through properly).

Then, Chloliet is really sad that I have run away and Stuart Hants insists that Chloliet start dating Ed Jonesio who is a member of the Poo Crew (and who Chloliet really hates) and asks her best friend Wumonia (I'm making that up) what to do and she comes up with a plan. She gives Chloliet a potion and tells her if she drinks it then she will fall asleep but everyone will think she is dead and she won't have to date Ed Jonesio (clearly Wumonia is an idiot and should never be listened to... EVER!).

But, Chloliet agrees to the plan and everyone thinks she is dead and when I hear the news I rush to be by her side and I am so sad that I can't go on without her and so I too drink a potion but my potion is POISON and I die (I'm still writing, so I'm not dead OK, IT'S NOT REAL!) but then Chloliet wakes up because she has only been asleep and sees that I'm dead and she is so sad she decides to be

dead too.

And there you have it. A very sad story of two people in love who die unnecessarily and a boy who poos his pants.

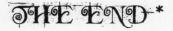

(*of Tedio and Chloliet, not my story)

So now you understand the story and can see why it was such a popular classic, can't you?

CHAPTER 18

When we arrived at the **GLOBE THEATRE**, I was amazed to see a *beautiful*, black and white, wooden building. It was round like a doughnut, but not as tasty. (I presume – I didn't actually lick the theatre to find out and, if you visit it in LONDON, I suggest you DON'T lick it either. To be honest, if you are the sort of person that goes to a theatre and licks the walls in the hope of them tasting like a doughnut, then you have been misled as to what a theatre is!)

There were lots of people queuing to get in. The RICH and the poor lined up in different areas. If you were rich, you could afford a cosy seat under the roof. The poor people stood in the middle and, if it rained, got wet.

William took my arm and guided me through the noisy crowds. He nodded to a woman at the entrance and after a brief conversation she allowed us both in. We took a seat with the POSH PEOPLE and waited for the play to begin. Here's what I noticed:

- Very few people paid attention to what was going on. They ate, talked and WALKED AROUND. It was like a whole-school assembly, but the roof was open so it smelled better!
- The audience that were paying

attention *cheered*, **booed** *and even* **threw** fruit and vegetables at the actors if they didn't like them or didn't like the characters they were playing. It was very interactive. (I think this should be introduced at our school. A few weeks ago, Year 2 did a presentation on what they learned on a geography field trip, which – for some reason – involved playing an awful tune on the recorder. If I'd had a tomato or banana handy, I would have definitely thrown it at them to make them stop.

I thought being at this play was quite EXCITING and, even though I didn't know what was going on, I stood up and cheered. 'Hooray!' I shouted at the top of my voice.

William looked at me and GLARED, as did all the people around me. 'Why are you cheering?'

'I don't know. I got excited,' I answered. 'WELL DON'T, this is a very sad and serious part of the play.'

'Is that why everyone is **booing** the actors?' I asked, hearing a loud noise from the crowd.

'They are not booing the actors,' replied Shakespeare who had turned red with embarrassment. 'They are booing YOU!'

Sure enough, everyone was now facing me. They all looked very angry. Suddenly, a piece of fruit came flying over people's heads and landed at my feet. Followed by a soggy cabbage that hit me on the shoulder.

'What's happening?' I asked.

'You cheered the BAD GUY. No one cheers

the bad guy! They are upset with you.'

I looked around and the whole crowd were holding various **mouldy** fruits and vegetables and looking right at me. They raised their arms and all at once launched the produce into the air in my direction.

I quickly shut my eyes, pumped my fist up and down and VANISHED.

I arrived back in my bathroom, pulled on my socks and rushed into the hallway, nearly knocking over my mum who was carrying a huge pile of clothes.

'Hey! Be careful young man. I've just done the laundry!' she yelled. 'And what is that?' She said pointing at my shoulder. I looked down and noticed a big browny-green mess all over me.

'Umm, it's... cabbage.'

'How did you get covered in CABBAGE?'

'I must've dropped it at lunch.'

'Can't you eat properly?'

'I thought I could, but I guess not.'

'Take it off. I'll wash it quickly or it will stain.' (I didn't want to tell her that it had technically been there a few hundred years already!)

'Thanks, Mum,' I said, pulling off my shirt and throwing it to her. It landed on the pile she was carrying.

'Not on the CLEAN CLOTHES! Honestl,y it would be less messy if we lived with a **HIPPO.**'

'Can we get a hippo?' I asked hopefully.

'No, Ted, we are not getting a hippo. Are you going to clean up after it poops?'

'Nope, it was your idea. You have to do it.' I laughed and ran into my room.

Right, time to practise being an actor.

At least if I'm rubbish, they won't throw rotten food at me. Although, it also means Chloe will see I'm a rubbish actor and all my hard work convincing her I'm nice and caring and would make an excellent boyfriend would all have been a waste of time. So, I'm going to learn some lines. I'll meet you back here in a little while.

(Off you go!)

NEWSFLASH

• • BREAKING NEWS • • • BREAKING NEWS • • • BREAKING NEWS • • • BREAKING NEWS •

CHAPTER 19

WE INTERRUPT THIS BOOK TO BRING YOU AN IMPORTANT NEWSFLASH

BOM BOM

Newsreader: This is the news!

BOM BOM BOM BOM

Newsreader: News just in. It has been revealed that Chloe Onions will be unable to take the role of Juliet in the Stage Mount School production of *Romeo & Juliet*. After suffering a recent injury to her ankle, she has had to pull out of the role. In a written statement to the school, Mr & Mrs Onions explained, 'Chloe is very disappointed not to be able to take the role but wishes the rest of the cast lots of luck.'

The role will now be taken by her understudy, Faith Brook.

That was the news…

BOM BOM BOM BOM

WHY WON'T
YOU LOVE ME?

CHAPTER 20

After hearing the news that Chloe wasn't going to play *Juliet*, I was obviously disappointed. This was my one opportunity to hang out with her without **Sandy Bum** getting in the way. But I couldn't just drop out of the play because Chloe wasn't going to be in it.

Rehearsing with *Faith* was fun, she was always trying to make me laugh in the serious bits — until we both got told off, which made us **laugh** even more.

The next few weeks seemed to pass quite quickly. I didn't time travel, I just went to school, came home and stayed in my room going OVER and OVER the lines. Rehearsals went well until I had to pretend to KISS Faith which made all the other cast say, 'ooo♡♡♡♡♡ooo♡♡♡hh!' every time I went to give her a kiss. (which I didn't actually do because... you know... yuck and all that!) It didn't help that Mr Peters kept telling me to be more convincing that I was in love. Then Faith punched me in the arm, laughed and said, 'Yeah, Ted, be more convincing that you are in love with me.' And then she wailed, 'WHY WON'T YOU LOVE ME?' and pretended to cry really loudly, which made everyone laugh and made me blush and that made everyone believe that I did like Faith, which is confusing because

she is really nice and pretty and funny but...
you know... Chloe. So, everything is really
confusing at the moment and I'm trying to
be a really professional actor but it's so
difficult and I think I need to lie down and
think about STUFF.

Eventually, I started to forget about the
COMPLICATED GIRLS in my class
and started to remember my lines. Once I'd
remembered them all (there were a lot – did
you know the word 'love' appears ONE
HUNDRED AND FIFTY times in
Romeo & Juliet? That's a lot of love)
(I just checked, and so far I've written it 29
times in this book, but some of them were from
my mum so they don't count. I also checked and
I've written the word poo 26 times (27 now).
(poo, poo) There, now they are equal).

Anyway, every single day after school,

all the cast met in the main hall and we practised over and over again. Once I knew the lines well enough, I could concentrate on my acting and I tried to remember everything that Shakespeare had taught me. In the end I was pretty good.

'You are pretty good,' said Faith after our final rehearsal. (See, I told you!)

'Thanks. You too,' I said even though she was only OK. I didn't want to tell her that because she liked me, and I didn't want to spoil that (even though I only like Chloe).

(There are a lot of brackets in this bit aren't there?)

(**Yes!**) ↰
(That's your answer.)

Chloe eventually did come back to school and I could tell that she was disappointed about not being in the show. Especially when

I asked her if she was disappointed about not being in the show and she said, 'YES'.

Actually, I think, even though her leg was in PLASTER, she should've still played the part of *Juliet*.

We could've just rewritten the play a little bit. I'm sure **Shakespeare** wouldn't have minded. Here are my suggestions:

Romeo & Juliet
A play by William Shakespeare
Rewritten by Ted Jones

'Parting is such sweet sorrow that I shall say goodnight till it be morrow.
I see you are having trouble getting up.
I have a stick you can borrow.'

Or maybe...

'But, soft! what light through yonder
window breaks?
It is the east, and Juliet the sun.
With your leg in plaster,
you should walk, not run.'

Or how about...

'Romeo, Romeo, wherefore art thou
Romeo?
My leg is really itchy
Do you have a scratcher I can borrow?'

Maybe, maybe not. Anyway, back to
talking about Chloe. I didn't chat to her
much as she was getting a lot of attention.
She did however let everyone sign her

PLASTER CAST, which I was excited
about and thought for ages about what
clever thing I could write but, when I did get
my hands on the pen, it turned into a

DISASTER!

Why? (Reader)

Well, I'll tell you if you promise not to laugh.
Promise?

I'd like you to say, **'I promise not to laugh
because whatever you are going to tell me
definitely isn't funny.'**

...

...

...

OK then.

When *Chloe* came back to school, she
let everyone sign her cast. I couldn't think
of anything funny and I was too scared to

write anything SOPPY so instead I went for a very sensible, nice message. I wrote:

I wish you a speedy recovery. From Ted

But, just as I finished writing it, **Martin Harris** barged me out of the way and snatched the pen from my hand. He started to write, and was CHUCKLING to himself but no one could see what he was writing as he was covering it with his arm. When he had finished, he dropped the pen on the floor and walked off laughing. Everyone crowded around to see what he'd written.

HERE COMES THE DISASTER BIT!!!

Instead of writing his own message, he had changed mine, which now read:

I ~~wish you a~~ speed ~~recovery~~. From Ted

Yes, that's right, my message now reads, 'I peed. From Ted.'

Everyone was laughing. (Except you right?

210

Because you PROMISED!)

I know I should have just walked away
with my head held high, but I couldn't let that
go. Somehow, I wanted to get my **REVENGE**
and fortunately, after the final rehearsal,
an opportunity arose which was too good
to miss.

Stand by, everyone. Ted is
about to get his own back!

CHAPTER 21

After the final dress rehearsal (which means
you have to wear your costume not that you
have to rehearse whilst wearing a dress...
unless, of course, your costume IS a dress...),
I went to the drama room to change. I have
to wear a frilly shirt, a long waistcoat, boots
and hat with a feather in it. The only
other person in the drama room was Mr
Peters who was busy **TYPING ON HIS
COMPUTER.**

Suddenly, he tutted loudly. 'I've run out of

paper so I can't print. Don't let anyone mess around in here, Ted. I'll be right back.' And with that he rushed off.

I couldn't resist being **a bit nosey** and peered over at the computer screen and there it was! **THE COMPUTER SCREEN!** I'm kidding, I just said that to add ᗪᖇᗩᗰᗩ to the drama in the drama room.

On the screen was the programme for the show. It had a page about the play, a paragraph about Shakespeare written by a pupil in Year 5 and a cast list – everyone involved in the play was on the list. This was my opportunity. But I needed to be quick. I SC
RO
LL
ED
down the list of names and there it was...

Martin Harris.

I double-checked no one was coming and quickly changed the M to F, so the programme now read:

Background............. **Fartin Harris**

There you go, Fartin Harris. **REVENGE** is sweet. I rushed back and innocently carried on changing just as Mr Peters came in carrying a large pile of blank paper. He loaded the printer and pressed print. The deed was done. There was no going back now.

That evening I stood to the side of the stage and peered out through a gap in the curtain and watched as the parents, teachers and guests **filled** the hall. I saw a few of them look at the programme and laugh. Did I feel guilty? No!

Should I feel guilty?

Maybe a teeny, tiny little bit. But... NO!

I saw my mum and dad arrive and watched as they changed seats 32 times before deciding on where to sit! I waited until I saw Chloe arrive. She limped in and took a seat at the front. Even with her leg in plaster, she was beautiful. Even with a message written in big letters on her cast that now read 'I peed. From Ted', she was beautiful (if I didn't look at the message). I watched as she picked up the programme and looked through it. I waited until I saw her start to laugh and point out the line to her parents, who also laughed. I couldn't enjoy the moment for too long as I was barged out of the way by Martin, who stormed past me, jumped off the stage, picked up a programme from the nearest seat and looked through it.

He let out a kind of AARRRGGGGHHH!

noise. Or it might've been more like

EEEGGGGHHHHAAAA!

(I'm not sure, I was laughing too much).

REVENGE was super sweet. It was now

time to blow everyone away with my superb

acting.

I'm not going to give you a blow-by-blow

account of how the show went. So instead,

here are the HIGHLIGHTS.

* We started five minutes late because

Stuart Hans (AKA Stu Pants Poo

Pants) was in the toilet. We would've

started on time if he would've just

pooed his pants like normal (Note: As far

as I know, Stuart hasn't ACTUALLY ever

pooed his pants but I still say he does

because it rhymes and it's funny).

* At the end of part one, everyone stood up and clapped. Chloe tried to stand up but it took her so long that by the time she was up, everyone else was sitting down again and she didn't get a chance to clap so she just sat down looking embarrassed.

* After the interval, we had to stand in the middle of the stage so that the audience could see us because the girl in charge of the SPOTLIGHT had fallen asleep. She eventually woke up and Mr Peters told her off.

* As I bent down to 'kiss' Faith (not really, just acting) she sneezed in my face. Yes, actually sneezed in my actual face. The romantic moment was reduced a fair bit as I wiped the

SALIVA and **SNOT** away. The audience found it very funny. Later on, when Mr Peters was telling us how good we all were, he renamed the show *Romeo* and **Achooo**-liet (which annoyed me because I didn't think of it. If I had've thought of it, it would've been hilarious and clever and brilliant but I didn't, so it's not).

* It's **SNOT** HAHAHAHA!

At the end of the show, after we had taken our bows and everyone involved in the play was excitedly celebrating in the drama room, I slipped away to see if I could find *Chloe.* The main hall was emptying out, but limping towards me was my future wife (Chloe — just in case you didn't guess who I was talking about).

'Hey, Chloe,' I said a little more shyly than I

had hoped.

'You were really good.'

'So were you,' I grinned. Yes, it's true I actually said the words 'so were you' to someone sitting **watching** the show.

Chloe giggled. 'Oh, and thanks for coming to visit me in hospital last week. It was really **nice** of you. Sorry about Sandra, she can be a bit **moody** at times.'

I just blushed and smiled. She smiled back. She looked so beautiful and then she leaned in a bit closer to me as if she was going to give me a kiss.

AN ACTUAL KISS!
From **Chloe!**

I moved a little closer to her.

We were almost at kissing distance

When...

'Oi! Jones. I've been looking for you!'

NOOOOOOOOOO!!!!
MARTIN HARRIS!

'Did **YOU** change the words in the programme?' he yelled, **POKING** me in the chest.

'I don't know **what** you are talking about. Changed your name to what?' I protested.

'Someone changed my name from Martin to **FARTIN!**' he snarled, grabbing me by the collar of my shirt.

'**No way!**' I replied, trying not to laugh. 'That's **AWFUL!**'

'You aren't laughing, **ARE YOU?**' he said, coming way too close to my face. Even closer than Chloe had been. I was in danger of having my first **kiss** with Martin Harris!

'No,' I squeaked. 'There's nothing funny about the name **FARTIN.**'

'MY NAME'S MARTIN!'

'That's what I meant. It wasn't me, I was in rehearsals all the time. There is no way I could've changed your name to Fartin.'

'STOP CALLING ME FARTIN. And why are you so close to my face?'

'Sorry, but you're the one holding my shirt collar.'

'Are you trying kiss me as well as Chloe? Right, well when I find out who changed my name they are in **BIG** trouble!' And with that he stormed off shouting, **'TED JUST TRIED TO KISS ME!'** to anyone that would listen (which thankfully was no one). I quickly swung round but *Chloe* WAS GONE.

NOOOOOOOOOO!!!!
WHHHHHHHY DOES THIS HAPPEN
EVERY TIIIIIMMMEE??!!

(If this were a movie I would drop to my knees and the camera would zoom up into the sky while I shouted NOOOOOOOOOO! But it's not, so I didn't. But I felt like it).

I sighed heavily and turned back around ready to head back to the drama room, but standing in front of me was *Faith*.

'Are you OK?' she asked.

'Yes, I'm fine, just a slight situation with Martin Harris.'

'Oh, he's really annoyed. Someone changed his name from—'

'Yes, I know.' I interrupted.

'I wouldn't like to be the person that did it when he finds out who it was!'

'Sure, me neither.' I said, **nervously**.

'Well, anyway, I just wanted to say sorry for sneezing in your face. I think some **dust** from the costumes got up my nose and I couldn't help it.'

'It's fine, think no more about it,' I said.

'But I do, because I never got the chance to do this...' and with that she leaned in and kissed me.

ACTUALLY

KiSSED... ME!

My first kiss and it wasn't with Chloe! ARRGGGHH!!!!!!!!

Faith stopped kissing me and I just stood there, too shocked to move. She *giggled* and skipped off back to the classroom leaving me in the hall not able to move. MY. FIRST. KISS. AND. IT. WASN'T. WITH. CHLOE!

What do I do now?*

*In case you are as confused as I am at this moment, I'll try and explain:

It appears that Chloe likes me and I like-like her, but then Faith, who I like but not like-like, like-likes me. Got it? Good. Let's stop, take stock and think about all of this because my heart is beating FAST, my stomach is churning, my hands are SHAKING and I don't know what to do!

OK, here are some REEEALLY IMPORTANT RULES that I must now tell you. A few things have happened in the last few minutes and only you and I know about them. I need you to keep them to yourself.

DON'T TELL ANYONE!

That includes: **friends, relations, pets, pen-pals, social media contacts, news reporters,**

presidents, kings and queens.

1. DO NOT tell anyone that *Chloe* and I nearly kissed.

2. DO NOT tell Martin Harris that I changed his name in the programme to FARTIN HARRIS (I didn't need to say it again then but I wanted to, because it's so funny) (best thing I've ever done... EVER).

3. DO NOT tell anyone that *Faith* kissed me. **EVER.**

PROMISE?

• • •

OK then. Because things have got a little weird right now and I need to think this through. What is happening with *Chloe?* What just happened with *Faith?* What will happen if **Martin** finds out it was me that changed his name?

One thing's for sure, I think life is going to get a lot more **complicated** for me. The drama is only just beginning and I'm going to be taking a lot more trips to the toilet.

(This is a dramatic end to the story and NOT an indication that I will eat something bad and end up with diarrhoea.)

Hang on. I think I need to rethink this bit. I wanted this book to end on a cliffhanger not an image of me sitting on the toilet with a **BAD TUMMY.**

Hold on. One more try...

Rewind...

FRRRLLLLLLWWWLLLLPPPP

Annnnnddddd... ACTION!

...One thing's for sure, life is going to get a lot more **complicated** for **Ted Jones.** The drama is only just beginning and his **TIME-TRAVELLING** toilet may be his only hope!

(Ooh I like that. Very dramatic. The excitement has given me **goose pimples.** Do geese actually have pimples? I don't think they do. **Get your Google out** and look it up!)

Well, that's it for now, but keep reading for an *exclusive* sneak preview of my next exciting adventure!

First there's a bit to tell you about what happens and then I'll let you read a bit of the first chapter. **FOR FREE!** The rest will be available soon, but you'll have to buy that. (How else am I going to afford to buy Chloe chocolates and flowers?)

Enjoy!

TED AND HIS TIME-TRAVELLING TOILET

OH NO, PHARAOH!

Ted spends a lot of time in his toilet. No, you read that right. IN his toilet. But you would too if yours time travelled like his! So far, Ted has utilised his most unique utility to travel and ask advice from Roman centurions, Henry VIII, Neil Armstrong (though that was a mistake – blame Olllie for that one!) and Shakespeare. But when his teacher makes an announcement about a Very Exciting Thing, Ted isn't interested. That is, until he learns his name nemesis, Ed is...

CHAPTER 1

The day began with triple English.

Errgh! Why triple?

Nothing good ever happens in threes! Except the three-legged race (fun), scoring a hat-trick in football (never done it) and the three flavours of Neapolitan ice cream (strawberry, vanilla and chocolate — strawberry is the best).

Anyway, we had to write down what our parents did for a living and if we'd like to have that job and why.

After we'd been *furiously writing* for about ten minutes, the teacher clapped her hands to get the attention of the class and told us that she was going to choose people to read out their work. She chose my best friend Ollie first. He told the class that his dad was a nurse, which he didn't want to be when he was older because he didn't like HOSPITALS. I asked him why not?

'They make me sleepy,' he replied.

'Sleepy?' I asked

'It's all those beds,' he replied and then yawned, which made me yawn.

Yawning is contagious. Just try it. When you're in a room with other people, pretend to yawn*.

*Although don't do it in front of your teacher when they're explaining something that they think is really interesting — that would be rude (but funny — but mostly rude — but still a bit funny). But next time you are with people, pretend to yawn and see what happens.

I bet they copy you. **IMAGINE** being the **FIRST PERSON EVER** to yawn and it's that one *yawn* that has passed from person to person all around the world for **EVER AND EVER** since! That's crazy.

Ooh! Imagine you were the first person in the whole world ever to do a *PARP!* What would you think just happened? You'd probably think, 'UH OH! SOMETHING JUST FELL OUT OF MY BUM!' and then you would check and see that **NOTHING** was there and then you'd believe that you can shoot **INVISIBLE RAYS** out of your bum, which you'd think was super cool.

Note to self: Write to the people that make movies and sell them the idea of a superhero that shoots invisible rays out of their bum.

Actually, scrap that, I don't think they would buy it.

Back in class, Miss Simon was trying to get us to be quiet by telling us she had an **IMPORTANT ANNOUNCEMENT.** Teachers never have anything important to announce... ever!

'For the FIRST TIME in the history of Stage Mount School...' she paused for effect, '...we will be choosing a Head Boy and a Head Girl.'

There was an excited gasp that ran around the classroom.

Later on that day, I was walking through the corridor thinking about the Head Boy role. It sounded tempting but one thing I had decided was that I needed to lie low this term after all the excitement last term with the nearly kissing Chloe, and being kissed by Faith, and the Fartin Harris thing... so I definitely WASN'T going to stand as head boy.

'Hi, Ted!' called out Ollie as he ran and caught me up. 'Have you heard? Ed Jones and Stuart Hants are both standing for **Head Boy...**'

Sigh Well I can't let that happen, can I?

ABOUT THE AUTHOR

Steven Vinacour writes and directs TV shows and adverts and owns a content creation company, creating content for people who want content creating.

He likes skateboarding, dogs, magic, going to the gym, eating, and writing books about toilets (but not all at the same time).

He can't sing, plays football badly, his dancing abilities are questionable and he's not very good at being an adult.

Steven doesn't take life seriously enough and probably should know better.

GET IN TOUCH!

Ted **loves** to hear from you. If there is something you really want to know, really, **really** want to ask or really, **really**, **really** want to tell him then send him an email, and as soon as he gets back from **TIME TRAVELLING**, he'll reply.
www.tedstoilet.co.uk
Email: **tedstoilet@mail.com**

Or follow Steven Vinacour on Instagram where you'll find news, tour dates and silliness. **@stevenvinacourauthor**

Who knows? Maybe you'll see your message or question in a future story of

READERS' THOUGHTS

'Funny, funny, funny! This book is very funny! I found myself laughing, smirking, giggling, smiling at every page as it is so packed full of jokes, amusing situations and silly sounding sentences.'
Review on Toppsa

When I read your review, I couldn't find your name so (inspired by your great use of verbs) I found myself clueless, uninformed, unaware and unclear — but thank you, thank you, thank you! And also thank you!

'This book was very funny. I liked it because it was so silly that Ted can travel through time in a toilet.'
Karatekid

Well, Karatekid, I would argue that

my life is definitely not silly, it's complicated and frustrating (especially with Chloe) but I've decided not to argue as you are clearly a martial arts expert.

'We loved this book so much when we read it with our grandma. She couldn't stop laughing (literally, she was in tears).'

I, D & A

I am delighted that your grandma couldn't stop laughing but the fact that she was in tears bothers me. I don't want to be known as 'Ted the boy that makes grandmas cry'. Help her to stop crying by reading her a really boring unfunny book. How about trying one by ███████████?

[Name of author deleted for legal reasons.]

THANKS

I hope you enjoyed reading Ted's third adventure. Why not get in touch? Or, better still, leave a review online or even better, get in touch AND leave a review or even better leave a review, get in touch and then make up a song and dance routine using the words from the book.

Big thank you, once again to everyone that's helped spread the word by telling their friends about Ted. Special thanks to Jo, Chloe and Oliver, for checking everything before I send it to Fiona and Anna who then double check everything before you read it.

Finally, thank you to all the schools that I have Zoomed with. I can't wait to get back out and meet you all in person!

Don't miss **Ted's** other *AMAZING*
TIME-TRAVELLING **TOILET**
ADVENTURES!

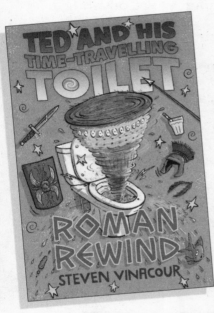

ISBN 978-1-78270-384-6

ISBN 978-1-78270-385-3